SOMETIMES I PREFER TO FUSS

Verda Peet

 AN OMF BOOK

OMF BOOKS are distributed by
OMF, 404 South Church Street,
Robesonia, Pa. 19551, USA;
OMF, Belmont, The Vine,
Sevenoaks, Kent, TN13 3TZ,
UK; OMF, PO Box 177, Kew
East, Victoria 3102, Australia,
and other OMF offices.

Published by Overseas Missionary Fellowship (IHQ)
Ltd., 2 Cluny Road, Singapore 1025, Republic of
Singapore, and printed by Singapore National Printers
(Pte.) Ltd.

Contents

Introduction

MY FIRST GLIMPSE of the mountain people of North Thailand was when they were performing their tribal dances for some VIPs from Bangkok. By tribal standards the Lisu are wealthy and they certainly commanded the most attention, with the men decked out in vivid green or blue satin baggy trousers, their black velvet jackets shining with silver ornaments. Tribal people are small in stature but one young Lisu dancer had the bearing of a proud young prince.

The Yao men were drab by comparison, but the red tufted wool collars on the women's jackets and their beautifully embroidered trousers added color to the Yao presentation. The Yao do not have a distinctive dance so they staged a mock wedding. The Akha, least affluent of the groups, sported no new clothes and were just scruffy looking, but the women's headdress adorned with silver coins, beads, chicken feathers, monkey fur dyed red, jungle seeds and shiny blue-black beetles gave an exotic touch. The Lahu, with whom we planned to work, were the least presentable, for their bright colored bands of cloth sewn by hand on their dark garments were faded by the sun and grimy from long use.

That day in 1953 we had no language to talk with them, but there was opportunity to play Gospel Recordings records in some of the tribal languages. For most of the listeners this was their first hearing of God's Good News.

I had never even thought of going to Thailand. My Canadian parents spent a brief missionary term in the Orient and as a small girl I said I too wanted to be a missionary to China. It was a childish fancy and soon forgotten, especially in my teenage years when missionary work seemed unimportant in my world of music and books. I did not then understand that a missionary is one with a message. I had no message, no Good News. I had a "religion", of course, but it was burdensome and did nothing to help my sense of something lacking in my life. Not until I was 18 did I see that "religion" was fruitless. What God offered me (and what He offers to anyone who will humble himself to receive) was not "religion" but a relationship with Him through faith in His Son. He took me into His family and helped me to see that obedience to His wishes was my privilege and my responsibility. So I left my piano teaching and went to Bible School, where China again claimed my interest.

I expected to spend my life there, probably in single blessedness. I did not foresee that the Communists would come into power and that four and a half years would be the limit of my China experience. It was because of the Communists that the American — Larry — who was to become my husband was not allowed to come to Chefoo School where I was teaching, so our wedding had to wait till after we left China in 1951.

The mission we belonged to changed its name from China Inland Mission to Overseas Missionary Fellowship and began to send missionaries to various Asian countries, including Thailand. Our knowledge of the land once called Siam was meager, but we did know there were tribal people there. So in March 1953, with our five-month-old baby Marilyn, we left on a freighter for Thailand. In due time a second daughter, Shirley, and two sons Gordon and Alan came to complete our family.

In North Thailand there are well over 300,000 tribal people, and the Overseas Missionary Fellowship takes responsibility for about half that number; the Sgaw Karen with 30,000 and Pwo Karen with 17,000; the Blue Hmong (28,000) and White Hmong (15,000); the Yao estimated at 24,000, the Lisu with 15,000, and the Akha with 13,000. Another mission is now responsible for the 15,000 Lahu, and the 24,000 Shan in the north-western valleys are not a tribal people but related to the Thai.

150,000 people. I cannot visualize that impersonal number. It helps me to remember that God doesn't see them as a vague mass but knows them by name, people like Jer Sha and Mplia Dua and Txwj Npl Haib. He is not dismayed by these unpronounceable names. He knows their longings and their needs, the present physical ones and the eternally important ones. He also knows where they live. It would have been more convenient for the missionaries if these tribal people had lived close together in well-defined areas, instead of being scattered through hundreds of miles of mountains, often hidden in-out-of-the-way places in the high forests. But they are never hidden from Him.

This book is as factual as I can make it. I am now at that great and glorious age when I can recall what happened thirty years ago but not where I put my pen! But my memory has been aided by the official monthly reports from our mission, plus my own letters kept by my fond mother. My fellow missionaries have patiently put up with letters full of the questions "how?" and "why?"

This is not a historical or chronological survey, but is written topically, from my own personal viewpoint and doubtless biased by my Canadian background and melancholic temperament. Tournier says[1]: "When we evoke our memories we can never be sure we have banished all illusion from them however sincere we are. What we call to mind is not the facts themselves but their appearance, the way in which we saw and felt them. All we have seen and felt, images and sensations, remain more or less distorted in our memories." Facts are facts, but I take responsibility for my observations of these facts and the conclusions drawn from them.

A scatter-brained housekeeper who was always in a muddle about her accounts decided she really

---

[1]The Meaning of Persons.

must do some bookkeeping. At the end of her first week she accounted for her $20 as follows:

Peanuts for Mary — $0.10
Miscellaneous — $19.90

A large amount in the miscellaneous column is no help in accounting; and it is no help in praying either. We bunch everything together, expecting the Lord to sort it out, but if it is too vague we cannot tell if prayer has been answered or not. In the Lord's Prayer we are told to ask for definite things like food and forgiveness and protection from the evil one. "Lord bless the missionaries" is better than no prayer at all, but sometimes it is a lazy prayer, or just a salve to the conscience.

The idea that missionaries are haloed saints, mature and perfected, above the sins of most mortals and so not needing much prayer, has done great disservice to the missionary cause. If you ever lived with missionaries you would know that their haloes are askew. If I were to say that a missionary preaches the Gospel, may (if female) put curlers in her hair, likes ice-cream, travels a lot, longs for letters from home, can be thought-less or domineering or depressed, perspires, has cakes that don't always rise, never gets beyond the need of the Lord's teaching, is concerned about her children's upbringing and education and feels irritable in the heat, your first thought would be "Sounds like a description of me." Exactly. James tells us that Elijah was a man of like passions but we have trouble believing it. Our glamorization of missionaries blinds us to their need of down-to-earth prayer for down-to-earth details, and I hope that this book may break down some of our "miscellaneous" prayers into specific requests that God will answer.

Chapter 1

Measuring Cups

ONE DAY I baked two pies for a church get-together, and just before we left for the church I gave a sample to my husband. Normally Larry eats anything set before him without complaint, but this time he ate two mouthfuls and then quietly put the pie to one side. When I tasted it for myself, I pitched both pies into the garbage and went to the church social empty handed.

We had recently moved into a home of our own, after years of living in Mission Homes. We had to start from the beginning finding new kitchen furnishings, and to add to the muddle of those days of settling in I was having one culinary disaster after another. My non-fail recipes were failing. I have never considered myself a threat to the Cordon Bleu, but many things I prepared were edible and sometimes appetizing, and my husband and four children have survived my kitchen efforts! So I was puzzled.

Then one day I found out what was wrong. I had three different kinds of cups! I was using the Thai cup for milk, the American one for flour, and the British one for fat, and they were all different sizes, so of course my cooking flopped. It cheered me to discover a reason for that spoiled food, and pointed up the fact that different countries may have different sizes for measuring things. People differ, their standards of measurement differ and their ways of doing things differ. And when we go into a new culture we become very aware of the difference in the "measuring cups."

The American's first shock in Thailand is that traffic drives on the "wrong" side of the road. It takes a while to get used to, but it can become second nature, as proved by the missionary who failed his driving test in the States because he turned a corner and swung into the lane he would have used in Thailand. At your first Thai meal you must learn to use your cutlery properly. Your fork is for pushing purposes, and only your spoon goes in your mouth. It's simple, and easy for children to learn to do gracefully. No knife is necessary for the food is in bite-sized pieces, convenient for the diner but time-consuming for the poor cook who must spend a lot of time in the kitchen. We liked the Northern Thai custom of dispensing with spoons altogether; you roll the sticky rice into a ball and dip it into the savory side dishes. When I say "sticky rice", please don't picture a gluey mess of improperly cooked rice. It is a special variety of rice with short round kernels that requires a long steaming time, and it is delicious.

When you visit a Thai home, if no one is in sight and the dogs have not announced your arrival, you don't knock. You can cough, or if that doesn't help, you call out and ask if there is anyone home. In a Lahu village you would walk in, if the dogs allowed you to do so.

One of the nicest Thai customs is to take your shoes off inside the house. It is cool and comfortable to go barefoot, and it keeps the floor cleaner. On occasion your shoes may disappear, but that does not often happen. We wakened one morning to find that all the men's leather shoes placed on the Mission Home porch were gone. The ladies' sandals were still there. So it makes sense to bring your shoes in at night!

Customs like these are relatively unimportant. So far as I know, there is no particular reason for the way they are done. But with customs based on moral values, to err is of greater consequence.

For example, there are differing ways of showing displeasure. If you reprimand a Thai you must not look at him, for gazing off into the corner of the room makes the scolding less offensive. On the other hand, if you scold a Karen you *must* look at him; to avoid his eyes suggests you are too angry to face him. A Hmong doesn't need to state his disbelief, but just bites his bottom lip. How many an innocent Hmong has thought the missionary was not believing his story when the foreigner didn't even realize he was biting his lip? It is easy to give the wrong signals.

Standards of modesty in dress vary, too. We think it strange that nursing mothers and elderly ladies may, in their own homes, wear nothing but a skirt, while they think our sleeveless dresses are impolite. Akha skirts are very abbreviated and expose a vast display of midriff, but the Akha women are most particular about how they sit. When small Cornelia, living with her missionary parents in an Akha village, wore her first Akha clothes, the village women took pains to instruct her how to be modest. In no way could a White Hmong lady in her black baggy pants and leggings be accused of immodesty; but to be proper in Hmong eyes, she must also wear a long skinny apron with its beautifully embroidered belt tied at the back. One of our missionaries who has learned the intricate Hmong embroidery and is clever at designing new patterns, says she is often embarrassed because Hmong ladies want to admire and copy the patterns on her apron. She must then sit still till her apron is returned to her.

"When we Thais go abroad," said one Thai lady to a missionary friend, "we dress in our very best, and look as neat as we can. So what is wrong with these foreign hippies who are sloppy and dirty, and the women don't even wear proper underwear?" She interpreted this careless dress as disrespect for Thai standards. I know how she feels, for after a time the local standards become yours. I often hurried past tourists on the street, hoping the Thai wouldn't connect me with those thongs, shorts, and sundresses. In that land of black-haired dark-eyed people, I even found I experienced a slight sense of shock when I unexpectedly met a blonde with blue eyes. Someone once asked us why we didn't take our son Gordon to a doctor and have his blue eyes "repaired"!

In Thailand a person's head is regarded as sacred. Barbers used to apologize before starting to cut the patron's hair. Buddhist shrines and objects of veneration and pictures of royalty must be hung high on the wall, above other pictures. If it is necessary to go past people seated lower than you, it is polite to lower your head. I was in the American Consulate one day when two very tall GI's went for information to a Thai lady seated at a desk. She motioned for them to sit down, but the men, being polite in the American manner, continued to stand. She tried again but it didn't work so, with resignation over discourteous foreigners, she went on with the business in hand.

A few years ago, three young men representing a foreign religion visited some old ruins containing the remains of temples, Buddhas and other sacred objects. One of the men climbed up on a statue of Buddha, and had his picture taken sitting on the Buddha's shoulders. No one was around, and it would never have been known except that the photographer who developed the film was so incensed that he took the offensive picture to the authorities. The young men served a jail sentence. What would be a comparable insult in our homelands? Perhaps if a foreigner went into a cathedral and, with a cigarette dangling from his mouth, posed for a picture perched on a statue of the crucified Lord Jesus, this would come close to it. In Thailand this unforgiveable incident did nothing to redeem the portrait of "The Ugly American", and in a sense involved all missionaries, implying that we have no decency.

The Thai do not appreciate our western custom of shaking hands. Their own gesture of greeting, the *wai*, with palms meeting before the face and a slight inclination of the head, avoids the familiarity of touching a stranger. Some of this attitude is changing, due to Hollywood and more contact with the West, but any public show of affection between the sexes is not part of Thai culture. One of our missionaries was one big beam of joy as she went to meet her future husband at the church altar, but a close Thai friend whispered to her, "Don't smile like that!" She was afraid people might consider her shameless. Engaged couples must be very circumspect. In this whole area, the hearty, outgoing, backslapping Westerner doesn't show up well. In fact, we don't even walk properly. A Thai neighbor said to a missionary, "When you walk fast down our lane, people think you are angry." The brisk trot of a foreigner does not accord with the Thai ideal of a "cool heart."

If you were to tell someone you had injured your foot, you would apologize for mentioning this, for the feet are regarded as low. How I cringe when I see foreigners sprawled with their feet on a low coffee table in a hotel lobby! On a bus once we saw some tourists put a suitcase with tennis shoes tied on outside, on an overhead rack. People began to fuss, but the tourists didn't speak English so we could not explain. They moved the things rather unwillingly, for they had no clue what the confusion was all about.

We were once traveling on such a heavily-laden boat that there were no spare seats, and the owner gave me permission to lie down in a small sleeping area. I wondered where I should put my feet, for it didn't seem correct to have the soles of my feet pointing at the other passengers — so I lay down with my head pointing at them. But the boatmen immediately reacted, for I had put my feet where they put their heads, and this had offended them. For the rest of the journey, with each recollection of my *faux pas*, I felt guilty and embarrassed. It makes you ill at ease to be constantly wondering if you are about to commit another blunder, and underlines the urgent need of prayer that we will not be a hindrance to our message.

On that occasion I wanted to please but chose the wrong way to do it, and this is an area where East and West truly clash. You inquire when the bus is to leave. Obviously you want to leave right away, so the bus boy tells you what he thinks you want to hear and says "In a minute." By the time the "minute" has stretched to an hour and a half, you are fit to be tied, and angry at the prevarication of the bus boy. But wait. Behind all this lies the Buddhist doctrine of Right Speech: you must not say anything that will displease. The bus boy wants to please and gives what he thinks is a pleasing answer. He does not realize that the foreigner will regard it as a lie, and will be infuriated.

To have a "cool heart" is a Thai ideal. To remain poised and in control of the emotions, to strive to avoid any confrontation or outward dis-agreement, this is the attitude to cultivate. And this is something I used to puzzle over and feel hurt about. A girl house-helper would not come to work, and I would discover she had left her job. She gave no notice and it seemed so inconsiderate. But now I know she felt it was embarrassing to say, "It is no fun working for you, and I may get better pay somewhere else." Not appearing at work spared my feelings, and hers. These are the conflicts that come when the Westen regard for facts, punctuality, and fidelity to a contract meet the Eastern desire for smooth relationships and the avoiding of stress.

People from the East have much to teach us Westerners. They are remarkably patient in their troubles and have more than once been a silent rebuke to missionaries fussing over trifles. The tribal folk don't read helpful books on how to deal with stress. They have no psychologists to consult. They can't stop for tragedy, but get on with the business of living. I feel they know more than we do about harmonious relationships and about yielding to others in everyday living. They recognize there are differences in temperaments and don't feel critical of one who is different. They give the retarded their own place in the home and don't make them feel as if they do not belong. They can gracefully accept the small ills of life. You would not find a bus load of Thai fretting and fuming because the bus doesn't start on time — delays that would have a Westerner reacting madly are accepted with peace. I remember a 2 a.m. scene in a Los Angeles airport when our plane arrived hours late and nearly everyone missed their connecting flights. The hapless desk clerks were in no way responsible for the delay, but they had to take the abuse of the irate and voluble Americans. If the passengers had been Lahu they would have taken their packs off their backs, put them on the floor for pillows and stretched out happily for a sleep.

This desire to relate peacefully to everyone poses problems for us foreigners. Someone comes to borrow money from a Yao tribesman. He says he doesn't have any, though everyone knows he has silver buried under the house. A Thai Christian secretary said that if her boss suggested some unethical work she would say that she was too busy. This excuse tells the boss her reluctance, and he gets the message. The words, though not literally true, give the true meaning. In a similar way the Yao neighbor knew there was silver under the house, and understood his friend's answer to mean that he cannot, at that point, loan any money. This is not the way we Westerners get out of difficult situations.

Canadians Don and Margie Cormack were working such long hours that Margie attempted to get Don to take a day off once a week. This was not always possible, but even when they managed it folk would come to the house to find him. Margie did not want to turn people away but she knew that Don, who had had indifferent health, truly needed a change of pace. Taking her problem to her Christian language teacher, she asked, "What should I say to the people who come? Should I tell them Don is resting?"

"Oh no!" said the teacher emphatically. "That would make them feel as if they were unimportant and didn't matter. You must say he is sick, or he is out."

"But I can't say that if it is not true," protested Margie.

"Oh, they will know he is home, but they won't be offended if he doesn't tend to them," was her reassuring word.

We find this utterly mystifying. What we would regard as the truth would give offense, whereas what we would regard as a lie conveys the true message that Don would really like to see them but finds it impossible to do so. It is hard for us to understand their measuring cups, and it is equally difficult for them to understand ours. This kind of problem, which crops up all the time, is very wearing for the missionary who tends to see everything in black and white, while the people he serves seem to live in a gray world. But in our own culture also we evade truth. Someone asks me "How are you?" and I breezily answer "Fine." I do not give them a run-down on my arthritis or the noise in my ear. Well, sometimes I do, but I try to restrain myself from burdening a mere acquaintance with my small ills, though the temptation to do so increases with advancing years! "How are you?" isn't really a question but a greeting, and we understand this. So my answer is not a lie but a response to a greeting.

Church discipline is not easy for Asians, not because they can't differentiate between right and wrong, but because they feel a deep responsibility to maintain outward harmony. We missionaries see things we feel should be dealt with, but sometimes our attempts to do so are bluntly offensive. We need so much larger doses of tactfulness than we ordinarily possess, sympathetic insight into the reasons for our neighbors' evaluations, and the gumption to ask for the wisdom God freely promises to His children who don't know what to do.

There is more than one good way of doing things, and sometimes other peoples' measuring cups may be more useful than our own. It is essential to hold firmly to the standards that God presents in His Word, for there are absolutes therein. Inevitably there will be tensions. It is not easy to find, or maintain, the fine line between an understanding acceptance of the ways of others and your own conviction of truth. But the Lord is able to teach us what to do about unequal measuring cups.

Chapter 2

Why Doesn't Everybody Speak English?

A LITTLE GIRL prayed one night, "God, why did you make so many languages and have it so hard for people to talk to each other? Wouldn't it have been easier to have everyone speak English like you and me?" When you are floundering in your early days as a missionary you feel like asking that question. Our North Thailand missionaries must learn first Thai, then a tribal language. If you are from the continent of Europe, you must tackle English before you even join our English-speaking mission. Some hardy souls work at still another, for Northern Thai, though not completely distinct from Central Thai, is different in many ways, and knowing it is a help in country areas.

I grew up in a small prairie town where no one ever thought of French as a language to be "spoken." It was a matter of book work, of memorizing vocabulary, making up your own pronunciation as you went along, and translating interesting stories. My success in this deceived me into thinking that my next language could be an equally pleasurable experience. To my horror I found when I started Chinese that knowing something in a book had little to do with talking to people and understanding what they said. To sit down with a Chinese book and a dictionary was one thing. To be surrounded by Chinese and to be expected to say something wise, or even just to say something, was quite another.

I can still feel my sense of panic when my senior missionary and I made our first visits to the little country churches for weekend conferences. My senior was fluent in the language and the people loved her, and she would immediately be carried off by a group of Christians to talk over their affairs. And I would be left in the main courtyard, in the midst of the idle onlookers that always gathered when a Westerner appeared. They would hem me in, staring and generally silent, and the occasional remarks they made to each other didn't appear to be flattering. I couldn't run and I couldn't hide, though I wanted to do both, and the few sentences I knew didn't seem appropriate to be launched on that sea of faces.

When we talk about tribal languages, do you think of twitterings and mutterings and gestures that inadequately express primitive thought? No. These North Thailand languages are fully developed and complex. Akha, for instance, has about three dozen final words that have no meaning in themselves but serve to show if the speaker is angry, surprised or noncommittal, or whatever. There are three sets of these finals, one to be used when the subject is the speaker, another when the subject is the hearer, and still another if the subject is someone else. In speech you don't have time to sit and choose the apt word; you must be

able to use them automatically. The experts say
that Akha is of average difficulty; they rate Yao as
being more complex still. Yao has six significant
tones, but a lot of verbs and nouns have one tone
when they occur before a verb and another before
a noun. The innocent missionary must know the
tone, what tone it may change to, and when the
tonal change takes place.

We all know people who speak English with a
foreign accent, which may be charming, or irritating. Before I went to Thailand, a friend said to
me, "You will certainly have trouble with the
language; you have such a Canadian accent!" I felt
slightly wounded about this, especially as my
friend came from Kentucky and had an out-
rageous accent of her own. When we had new
missionaries living with us while studying Thai,
there were often English classes in our home. One
girl from England taught British English. One was
from Carolina so her Thai students cultivated a
southern accent. Another hailing from Vermont,
and still another, a German-speaking Swiss, also
shared their brands of English. We wondered
sometimes if their students were ever baffled
when they tried their English on each other! The
fact is we *all* have an accent, and we have to lose it
or people will be concentrating on how we say
things rather than what we say.

Did you ever realize that in English we say two
different kinds of "p"s? We all know how to
pronounce the "p" in the word *pout*. But if we put
an "s" in front of it and say *spout* that "p" sound is

changed. The little puff of air that comes with the "p" in *pout* is missing when you say *spout*. In English we do it automatically, not even knowing there is a difference, but in some languages that little puff of air, or its absence, is important. In Thai if you are telling someone to shut something and put in a puff of air that shouldn't be there, you would be telling them to sin. Many people have difficulty in hearing these differences, and then of course it is more difficult to pronounce them. I remember in China two missionaries having an amiable argument as to the correct pronunciation of a certain word in Chinese. Finally they decided to bring the cook in and ask him. They showed him the word they wanted pronounced and he said it. And with great triumph both of them said, "See, I told you so!" What made it funnier was the fact that we who listened heard that neither of them said it the way the cook did!

Nowadays the new missionary in Thailand goes to an excellent language school, but there is no language school for the tribal languages. Our linguistic experts have come up with many helpful ways of learning a tribal language, but it is never painless. One of the first snags is to find a teacher. That doesn't mean a trained teacher — they are rare birds indeed — but a national who is willing to help you learn to speak. He will likely approach the job with skepticism. After all, here is an adult having a terrible time to say things their infants say effortlessly. Is there any hope of teaching someone with such inadequate mental powers?

Our Lahu friends all agreed that our young Marilyn, who spoke good Lahu, was much brighter than her two still-struggling-with-the-language parents. Tribal folk are not used to sitting still for long, and the teacher gets sleepy and incredibly bored with the needed repetition of difficult sounds.

Even a pessimistic, bored, sleepy teacher is better than no teacher at all, and some of our young folk have not been able to hire anyone. Ted and Nell Hope could not move into a Lisu village where they wanted to be, and so went instead to a Karen Christian village as near to the Lisu as possible. They sent out an urgent request for prayer: for it is difficult for an Australian nurse (Nell) who speaks Thai and lives in a Karen community to try to learn Lisu from a Rhodesian (Ted)! It is in these down-to-earth situations that you find out if you really believe in the sovereignty of God.

The quicker the language student can form a friendship, the easier it will be. And if he can find someone willing to correct his mistakes, he has found a friend indeed. Easterners are polite. To correct you is to make you lose face, and they don't like to cause you this grief. Another helpful kind of friend is one who will *initiate* conversation. When I first lived in a Lahu village, my verbal powers were limited to a series of questions concerning family and relatives. After I had inquired as to the number of my neighbor's children and their ages, I was stuck. And there is a limit to the number of times you feel free to ask your nearest neighbor how old her kids are. I desperately wanted the neighbors to carry the conversational ball, but often they didn't. Those hateful awkward silences! But the pastor's wife had no time for silences. She forced me to talk, and if I couldn't understand her question she repeated it, or rephrased it, until I did. This need for a helpful language friend lies near the top of priority prayers.

Somewhere around is a language book called *Thai without Tears*, but it is a rare person who learns a language without a sniffle or two. I know one who breezed his way through language study, but he is gifted and outgoing and loves to talk. There is a relationship between personality and expertise in language. A person who is untalkative in English will be untalkative in Thai or Lisu. But even more basic is the matter of pride. Those of us who are insecure find it difficult to appear ridiculous. I always wanted to wait till I knew more or till my pronunciation was better before I'd say anything. But this is deadly. I have a friend who blunders along in two languages, her tones every which way and her final consonants exploding when they should be silent. But she communicates, and wherever she goes she makes a host of friends. When she chatters away in her inadequate Thai shopkeepers beam and respond, for they know she regards them as people and wants to be in touch. A proud perfectionist cannot do this. Maybe this is connected with the Tower of Babel, when pride incurred the judgement of God and resulted in confusion and multiplicity of tongues. Today a "Tower of Babel" ego can keep me bound, so that I am not free to lose face, appear childish and make real progress by profiting from my mistakes.

In language learning mistakes are inevitable. A lady at home prayed for Christians in a place she pronounced as "Sin-gap-aree." Folk were really confused until they realized it was the people from "Singapore" she was remembering. Tonal languages abound with opportunities for pronunciation mistakes. More than one housewife in Thailand has called for a doctor when she really wanted a cooking pot. In the confines of your own kitchen this does not matter, but in preaching it does. Someone wanted to speak of God who is the Almighty One. But by changing one tone, he described God as a large lady. Satan uses words to confuse the truth, to make it appear ridiculous, and to create misunderstanding. In the early days when we still used hand wound phonographs, a Karen record used an expression for Jesus which meant "half-wit." That has long since been corrected, but it is the type of thing Satan encourages in people's memories.

Learning a language affords many opportunities for also learning humility. When one of the missionaries to the Akha was beginning to give Bible studies in Akha, she told how in the prayer time preceding her message someone was likely to pray, "Lord, help us to understand what our teacher is going to say." It was hard to know whether to be put off at this reminder of her shortcomings, or pleased at their prayerful concern!

A Thai lady had come to our Lahu village to find me and get some medical help. She raced through her symptoms in Northern Thai, and I got a bit of it but knew I must understand it all if I was going to prescribe medicine. Managing to stop the flow of words, I hesitatingly asked her to say it again. This started her off in full spate. "Why, Pastor John (the missionary who preceded us) could understand Thai, Northern Thai, Yao, Lahu, and Akha, and he could speak them too!" There was no malice in her words; she was just giving me the facts as she saw them. I meekly agreed that Pastor John was indeed fabulous, and would she please repeat her symptoms, which she did. Such moments are given to us to keep us humble.

I have sometimes wondered if language learning was turning me into a hypocrite. To admit you don't understand everything brings the conversation to a complete stop, so instead you smile and look as intelligent as your facial features will allow, and hope you get enough of the gist of it to make a suitable reply. I am glad I don't know all the things I have given assent to in Thai and Lahu. If it is deceitful to pretend you understand more than you do, it seems to be a necessary part of getting on with things. A friend of mine as a small girl went to visit an old lady, and when she got home she convulsed her family by reporting that Mrs. X was very ill, but she still had her "facilities." Before we left Thailand for retirement I still had most of mine, but it is true that I was not hearing even English as clearly as I once did, so language "hypocrisy" seemed to be a necessity.

To jump from a satisfying ministry at home into a frustrating world where you use the vocabulary of a four year old, fumble for words, say what you *can* say and not what you *want* to say, feel clueless and lost, drowning in the conversational stream — this is for many a traumatic experience. During this period most missionaries have spells of thinking, "Maybe I should go home where I can say what ought to be said." It is hard not to be discouraged when it is impossible to *see* your language progress. It is like watching a tree grow. When we moved to a new house in Chiang Mai there was a small twig in the ground, so small we hardly noticed it. In a year it was big enough to shade our upstairs window. Though I saw it every day I never actually *saw* it grow. But it did.

We need courage to persevere until that day when we can, in our adopted language, "declare His glory among the nations, His marvelous deeds among all peoples." Our days of distress will lead somewhere if we have confidence that He intends for us to have enough words for the work He has in mind for us, enough words to describe Him who is God the Word.

Chapter 3

A New Song

MUSIC IS a universal language — nowhere in the world are there people who don't sing — but our expression of that music is not universal. There are many kinds, and we normally prefer that type with which we are familiar, which has arisen from our own culture and background. It is another case of measuring cups.

It was in China I first learned that many Easterners don't appreciate our western harmony. Seated at the organ in church I enjoyed my harmonies and elaborations, until a senior missionary informed me that the average country church member couldn't hear *any* melody when I played four parts. To them it was just a jumble of sound. So thereafter, though it took considerable restraint on my part, I played the tune in both hands an octave apart.

I also discovered that I found Chinese music difficult. Mr. Wang, one of our language teachers, had been asked to sing a classical Chinese song at a language school party. We were warned in advance that it would sound strange to us, and on no account were we to look amused. The warning was necessary, for our first reaction was to laugh. But the song was full of meaning to Mr. Wang, and our laughter would have sorely offended him.

Had we sung a choir number in English perhaps he would have felt just as confused.

Music has a deep emotional hold upon us, evoking memories and satisfying inner longings we may not be able to put into words. Our hymns have helped us to praise God and to grow in faith, and we can easily feel that a person who doesn't like our style of church music is unappreciative of spiritual things. But this is not so.

The music of these eastern cultures is based on a different scale from ours: the Chinese scale has five notes, the Thai has seven. So they find our music as distressing as we find theirs. Thai music does not ordinarily use harmonic chords, but concentrates on melody. In an orchestra this is carried by one instrument, with the others inter-weaving the melody, rather like an intricate round. Thai musicians are free to improvise. Our ears are accustomed to our own musical forms so we don't catch the Thai musical pattern. To us it seems to go on and on without getting anywhere, but to the Thai it is full of meaning.

Thai is a tonal language and with songs this presents a problem. If there is a rising tone at the end of a line, the melody must be adjusted to that. But in the second verse the word at the end might have a falling tone, and the tune must change slightly to fit that tonal pattern. So the tune of verse one may be sung in one way, and the tune of the second verse in another.

In fact, some of the tribes do have an ear for our style of harmony. The Lahu enjoyed all our classical records, gathering in our bamboo-walled house and listening appreciatively to Brahms, Beethoven and Handel. There was one exception, however. Our recording of coloratura Lily Pons singing the Bell Song from Lakme reduced them to helpless giggles. They tried valiantly to hide their amusement but it was "unhideable." Lisu, Akha and Lahu quickly learn our style of music and are able to sing in parts without any accompaniment, an accomplishment not readily attained by congregations at home! Often there was one book for ten people or so, and they would sit in a circle around it. It is quite a feat to read tenor upside down from a distance of three yards! For Lahu, Lisu and Akha Christians, choir practice has become part of the social life, an excellent replacement for the old non-Christian ways of amusement.

We sometimes helped teach music in the Akha Short Term Bible Schools, which involved laboriously writing out all the new music in four parts in tonic sol-fa. It says something for their expertise that they learned Stainer's "God so loved the world" in a five-day period, and in another such time they learned the Hallelujah Chorus. This last was not a polished performance but we had a lot of enjoyment from it, with Larry banging out the time with a ruler, me furiously pumping the organ and everyone singing as loudly and cheerfully as they could.

Early missionaries to Thailand wanted to share the things of God in music, and at first there were no Christians to help them use Thai forms of music. Not every missionary has the ability to compose music even in his own cultural style, so it is not to be wondered at if they floundered over Thai type of melody. They did the obvious thing, and translated our English hymns into Thai. The tribal missionaries did the same. The first small hymnbooks containing translations of western hymns were fairly well received. But after a while each tribal group began to "interpret" the tunes, and quite unconsciously the melodies changed. Due to Larry's duties we visited all our North Thailand missionaries, and it was fascinating to compare the Karen rendering of "What a Friend we have in Jesus" with the Hmong, Lisu, Yao, Akha and Lahu varieties. There were six different "flavors" to any one English hymn tune!

Every missionary has to come to terms with this. Westerners are meticulous and fussy and our great passion in life is to have things done correctly. There is a clear choice: you can fret and fume and make the Christians sing a hymn over and over again to get it right, bewildering them because they don't hear where they are wrong and don't understand what the fuss is about. Or you can relax, ignore your musical sensibilities, help the Christians to get the hymn correct in the first place and then let them enjoy it in their own fashion. The Word does exhort us to make "a joyful noise"!

There is another problem about using indigenous music, for most of it originally related either to demon worship or sex. When missionaries suggested using gourd pipes in church, the answer was an unqualified "No." Pipes recalled the days when they were used to invoke the blessing of the demons. There is no evil in a gourd pipe, but the association with the old, now forbidden, life was too strong. Because of these associations the early Christians had misgivings about their own melodic style, but gradually they have been helped to see that they can use their own musical heritage for God's glory.

For example, they use a ballad or chant type of music in their witnessing. Very early in the Hmong work Hmong Christians Ying and JaHu went on a preaching trip, and the crowds enjoyed tape-recorded preaching in the Hmong ballad style. It served as an introduction for Ying's hour and a half sermon, covering everything from Adam to Revelation! Recently a blind Hmong girl has applied an old Hmong story to Christian truth, and this is now on a cassette. The Shan have cassettes using their chanting style to tell of the Creation and Fall. These are very popular, especially in October, their big festival month, when everyone visits relatives and has time to sit and gossip and listen to the cassettes. There is even one in a Buddhist temple! An early Lisu ballad based on the blind man's story in John 9 ended: "I was blind and without a teacher, but now I have a teacher whom I have believed, and a guide whom I can trust (the missionaries). Behind my teacher there is a Teacher. Above my guide there is a Guide. God is the teacher's Teacher and God is the Guide of my guide."

These ballads are excellent in witnessing but are not suited for singing together in worship. In the meantime God had given to the Thai church musicians who could write poetry and set it to music, and gradually tribal words have been set to these Thai tunes. We pray for more musicians and poets among the tribal Christians, for there is so much of God's wonders to be shared in song.

The importance of music came to us so vividly the day we attended Ruth's recital before her graduation from university. Ruth is a young Thai Christian, now serving the Lord with her husband in North-east Thailand. On that occasion she sang beautifully from Handel, Bach, Rossini and contemporary composers. Finally, dressed in a lovely Northern Thai costume, she seated herself on the floor in traditional pose, surrounded by the Thai orchestra, and with simplicity and feeling sang Thai songs of praise to the Lord. Thai poetry set to Thai music by Thai Christians who have been taught by the Lord to sing a new song, is very moving. For music is the language of the heart. Our western hymns have been a help, but they are still foreign. The deepest experience of God's grace can best be sung in your own language, with words that spring from the heart, expressed in the kind of melodies known and loved from child-hood.

The Akha church is a singing church, for their leader is also a musician. A visitor who had heard

Britain's finest classical guitarists said that YaJu was the best amateur guitarist he had ever heard. Peter Nightingale and YaJu were once at a translator's conference where someone sang "How great Thou art!" This was new to YaJu and he liked it so after hearing one verse he leaned over and took Peter's pen from his pocket, and as the singer sang he recorded the music correctly! The festivities at one Akha Christmas celebration included the young people singing from house to house most of Christmas night and, during the worship service, the singing of an anthem written by YaJu. Every tribal Christian group needs people with musical gifts.

In 1954 two missionaries lived for a while in the Lisu village of Ta-ngo, but did not see anyone turn to the Lord. Nine years later one of them visited another Lisu village and was delighted to discover some old friends from Ta-ngo. But more than the delight of renewing acquaintance was the joy of having the teenagers gather round, eager to sing again all the songs they had learned as children. After nine years they were still remembering truth in song.

The tribal folk do have good memories. They could neither read nor write until the missionaries taught them so there was no way of jotting down things to be remembered. Information is either tucked away in someone's head or forgotten and lost. One elderly blind man who finally accepted God's way of salvation would tell people the story, recalling what different missionaries had talked to him about over a period of years. One had told him that God really loved him, another said that he needed the Lord in his blindness, someone else said he was old and must quickly believe. At the time he gave no indication that he received any of this witness, but it was all stored away in his mind like seeds awaiting the right time to germinate.

It was Amy Carmichael who said, "There is something immortal in seeds of song."[1] She tells the story of a young man who approached her one evening. "'Do you remember me? I used to come to the children's meeting under the tamarind tree.' And he chanted text after text and sang song after song. And I marvelled afresh at the power of life in the merest thistledown of song, and more and more we set words of eternal import to any simple tune we could find, and committed our seeds to the Winds of God." Many of the little old tribal ladies are convinced they will never be able to learn to read. Perhaps they are right. But even in their minds these musical seeds may lodge. They may never master printed truth, but they can sing and remember the One who is the Truth.

As long as I have been a Christian, the Lord has ministered to me in music. I have a battered old hymn book given to me in China some 35 years ago. It was from that book that we sang for the Communists. Things were tense under their rule. Communist soldiers had commandeered the front

---

[1]*Kohila*

building of our compound, and this made it easy for them to see who came to church and who visited the missionaries. By this time our visits to the believers were an embarrassment to them, so apart from short walks we were staying within our four walls. The soldiers didn't interfere with us; they were just there — and watching. One day their leader came to the house and said they had heard us singing, and wanted us to sing for them in English. We had little hope our English words would be understood, but we wanted a song that clearly expressed our faith. So next morning we moved the small portable organ to a space in front of the house and, after the soldiers had gathered round, we somewhat nervously started to sing:

"Look, ye saints, the sight is glorious,
See the Man of Sorrows now,
From the fight returned victorious.
Every knee to Him shall bow.
Crown Him, crown Him, angels crown Him,
Crowns become the victor's brow."

Perhaps it did nothing for them, but it did something for us. They were the victors, for certainly they were in command and not we. And yet we could sing with absolute certainty of our true Master, enthroned in the seat of power. We had had anxious moments at the time of the Communist takeover, and we had our times of fear about what the future might hold. But that morning, for me at least, God gave the certainty that He is King of kings and Lord of lords.

In times of discouragement or doubt, the Lord often brings to mind a snatch of something that restores me to faith. A short phrase from "How firm a foundation" has helped me through many a bad patch: "What more can He say than to you He hath said?" In the Lord Jesus He has fully spoken to all my needs. The tribal Christians have also found the Lord's comfort in song. Nineteen-year-old Doong had words with his mother one morning and left the house in a huff. He and his wife would normally have taken along a baby sitter for their two-year-old Mary, but feeling angered and wanting to escape they went by themselves to their field house, where Doong had been making bullets and had forgotten to put away the bags of gunpowder. They did not notice what Mary was playing with until there was a sudden explosion. They hurried the badly burned child into hospital, but she was beyond help. As Larry drove them home with their dead child, Doong wept and patted Mary's face, sorrowing all the more because he felt responsible for the accident. But he was able to turn to the Lord in his need, and at his request they sang as they traveled. "Does Jesus care when my heart is sad?" was one that helped to ease their pain.

For some time my husband and I were responsible for the tedious job of printing tribal literature: standing by a mimeograph machine turning out page after page of printed material that you can't even read, and walking round and round a long table assembling these pages into books. In some ways the circling is easier than the standing, and to stand or walk with a Mozart flute sonata echoing in your ears takes the drudgery out of it all. So many times when I was tearing my hair out with exasperation over a mimeograph machine that for no known reason would not cooperate, a hymn would bring peace:

"There is a hiding place,

A strong protective space,

Where God provides the grace to persevere."

Like people everywhere, missionaries have days when it is difficult to feel musical. How can we sing the Lord's song in a strange land? We just want to find some willows and hang up our harps. At such times I have found it helpful to make myself sing. It is not hypocritical if I say to Him, "Lord, I don't feel like singing, but I sing by faith because of the reality of Your presence and provision." A melody that starts as a deliberate act of will can turn into praise from the heart.

By faith, we can see the day when Shan and Yao, American and English, Akha and Karen, Lisu, Hmong and Lahu join the great and heavenly multitude singing, "Hallelujah, for the Lord our God, the Almighty reigns." We begin to learn the eternal song here and now; we sing it in our mundane and workaday lives. The Lord has made provision for us together to praise Him, witness to our faith and enjoy His presence in song. For He has designed us to become, as someone has described it, "walking arrangements of the Hallelujah Chorus."

Chapter 4

To Choose Our Garden's Weather

AT HOME IN Canada, seasons are sharply distinct. The first frosts turn the autumn leaves a rich red — at least I used to think it was the frost, though nowadays they tell me it has something to do with chlorophyll. Winter is a separate experience, and so is the melting of the snow and the first crocuses when the meadowlarks alert you to spring's arrival.

There is much less seasonal contrast in Thailand. The seasons tend to blur into each other, and you are mostly conscious of heat and greenery. Though trees do shed their leaves, you hardly notice this. Officially in Thailand there are three seasons — dry, hot and rainy. My own names for them are — dry and hot, extremely hot, and rainy and hot. "It is so hot in Bangkok that you want to take off your skin and sit round in your bones," said one friend. The book says: "Temperatures usually hover between 85° and 90° Fahrenheit (29°–32° Celsius), and temperatures above 100°F. (37°C.) are uncommon." I am not an authority so I must not disagree with this. But my personal thermostat registers more than 90° much of the time. One day when it was 108° in some-one's bedroom, she took the thermometer out in the sun and it shot up to 132°! Perhaps it is a

doubtful blessing having a thermometer to tell you
how hot you ought to feel!

In April I always went round with my face an
unbecoming shade of beet, without any exertion
whatsoever. But it was only foreigners, that is
Westerners, who looked hot. I used to marvel at
how calm and cool our Thai neighbors appeared,
looking better and complaining less than this
dripping crimson Westerner. The weather seems
to have little effect on the beautiful dark skin of
the Thai. They themselves prefer fair skin and
don't understand the American obsession for lying
in the sun to achieve the tan they naturally possess. Then foreigners go in for prickly heat. Our
small Peets often looked measly, and I once asked
my husband's Stateside family doctor what to do
about the children's prickly heat. "Keep them
cool and dry" was his infuriating advice, infuriating because of its impossibility.

90° weather is not horrendous, but combined
with 90% humidity it is. Thailand's air is often
saturated with water vapor so as to give the
impression of living in a perpetual steam bath.
When, on arrival in Thailand, we stepped out of
the pleasant air-conditioned plane into the humid
night air of Bangkok airport, we felt as if someone
had dropped a smothering blanket upon us. We
found seats in the airport bus and were driven to
the terminal, but the "blanket" didn't disappear
with the movement of air. Finally one of the
tourists said to a friend: "When we were coming
down the steps of the plane I thought I was feeling

the heat of the engines. I guess it's the climate here!"

Fellow missionaries home from Thailand were visiting a park with their two small sons. As they entered the greenhouse where the tropical plants were growing, the hot humid air enveloped them. "Oh," said one of the boys rapturously, "this is my favorite smell. This smells like Thailand!" Not all of us share his enthusiasm, for it is in the humidity that you perspire into your neighbor on a crowded bus, your arm sticks to your desk or your papers stick to your arm. It is impossible to study without a fan, and if you use one your papers fly all over the room. A very appropriate gift for a missionary in the tropics is a paper weight. You can never have too many.

I know I complained a lot about the heat, especially when darkness brought little reduction in temperature so that I wakened in the morning feeling as hot and tired as when I went to bed, as if it was a great mistake to start another day. Once, wondering if people who say they feel the heat just make more fuss about it than others who complain less and get on with the job, I consulted one of our mission doctors. She gave me a long and impressive list of things that can happen to you in the heat; circulatory instability, heat edema and salt depletion, ending with chronic tropical fatigue. Then she spoiled it by adding "Heat reduces the *willingness* to work rather than the *capacity* for work." This confirmed my suspicion that intolerance of heat is related to love of comfort. The more I want to be at ease the harder I find it to live in the tropics. It is extremely easy to be lazy and cantankerous in the heat, and it is a rare missionary who stays completely sanctified while the thermometer lingers in the 90°s. How much we need what Evelyn Underhill calls "an established temperature of God-given peace and joy, a climate of eternity at our center."[1]

Before I lived through a rainy season I imagined weeks of solid downpour like the occasional three-day soaker we would get in Saskatchewan. It isn't like that. It does rain furiously, then the sun comes out; it may rain again and the sun may shine, or it may stay cloudy. It is in the rainy season that you discover if wood has been properly seasoned, for doors, shutters and drawers tend to stick. Your envelopes glue themselves down before you use them, the salt won't come out of the shaker, and the frogs come into their own. We once had a frog choir under our bedroom window in Bangkok with a section of very low basses—basso profundo is the phrase that comes to mind. Then there were two sections of tenors, one pitched about three semitones higher than the other. The choir didn't croak every night, but they worked hard on the nights when they did perform. Once they tuned up about 10.30 p.m., rehearsed for a while then rested until the complete performance at 2.30 a.m., finishing off at 4.45. The alarm shrilling at 5.30 marked the end of an interesting night.

---

[1] *Fruit of the Spirit*

I looked forward to the rainy season because sometimes, for a few hours, the rain would bring some cooling relief. But most of us found the rains hard to bear in a mountain village where, when it isn't pouring, you can live in swirls of mist. A visit to your neighbor's house means slipping and slithering on muddy village paths made slick by rain and messy by pigs and chickens. It was humiliating to find that the constant dampness, the mold on walls and books and the unpleasant odor of washing that had taken three days to dry, was strangely depressing.

When we lived on the Laos side of the Mekhong River we usually did our marketing on the Thai side, so a shopping expedition included walking to a small landing place to find a boat going across, then climbing up fifty steep steps built into the river bank to the temple area at the top, and along a small lane to the local market. People talked about the Mekhong in flood but I could not picture it. How could that nine-hundred-yard-wide river in its deep gorge ever overflow? Then we saw it with our own eyes. There was no sign of the fifty steps that we so laboriously climbed in ordinary days. They were completely covered, and the boat docked by the temple wall. The river was one vast expanse of dark brown water, with logs and refuse swirling in its swift course. Many acres of rice crops were flooded, roads and bridges washed out, homes inundated and people drowned. We were thankful the flood water didn't reach our house.

Another year when we lived beside the river Ping, 150 miles south of Chiang Mai, it was a different story. Many Thai houses, especially in rural areas, are built up on stilts to avoid water damage, but our house at that time was only three feet above ground level. The rains had been heavy, and on Sunday morning there were spots in the road filled with waist deep water. The whole town was river watching, and although neighbors said no water had ever reached our house in previous floods, we kept getting up through the night. At 1 a.m. the yard was flooded and the water an inch from the floor. So we started moving the boxes and trunks belonging to missionaries in the hills. We first piled them on tables and furniture downstairs, but at 4.30 a.m. we began to cart everything, including the carriable furniture, upstairs. We put our charcoal stoves on the stair landing and moved upstairs ourselves to live in a glorious mess out of reach of the 22 inches of water downstairs. Larry had his picture taken on the front lawn with water up to his chin. Our four-year-old Shirley and three-year-old Gordon enjoyed the excitement of sailing down main street in a boat as they went to market each day with the househelp.

By Thursday morning the house was empty of water and, as Gordon commented, "God just put down His hand and squished it away, and now we have to clean up the muck!" We found baby poisonous snakes, scorpions, leeches, snails, fish, toads and frogs, both alive and dead, plus rotting

papaya, junk, and things we didn't care to identify. The water left a deposit of mud on the walls
inside and out. Everything had to be cleaned, and
it took days to restore order. Even so, we were
well off compared to our neighbors across the
street who lived for days on board planks they
erected just above water level. Everyone was
relieved when, after a week of doing without, the
electricity came on and the mail was delivered.
The Thai said never in living memory had there
been such a flood.

In the cool season in the north the days are hot
but you need a sheet and sometimes even a
blanket at night. Most foreigners enjoy it but the
locals feel the cold and really suffer. In Thai
villages in the early mornings you can see folk
huddled around small bonfires, towels or blankets
draped round their shoulders, waiting for the
mists to lift and take them out of their misery. But
on invigorating mornings, when the days are clear
and cool, you have to retract all the critical
thoughts about Thailand's weather. If climate is
the only thing you are concerned about, there are
days when you wouldn't want to be anywhere else.

A friend who helped in one of our homes for
retired missionaries before coming to Thailand
was impressed with the prayer ministry of the
elderly folk. But there was one oft-repeated
prayer that gave her pause. "Oh Lord, send the
missionaries breezes." Breezes? It seemed so
unspiritual. But after she had walked under the
tropical sun, plodding the mountains en route to

tribal villages, she hoped someone would continue to ask for breezes. And the Lord does send breezes, or else strength to go on, with some mind-expanding vista of distant mountains that you don't have to climb, just enjoy. He gives compensations for April's heat, like tangy mangoes and the gorgeous flame-of-the-forest trees, sometimes so covered with red blossoms that you feel it must be one gigantic flower. At times I miss these reminders of God's presence because I am too busy feeling sorry for myself. Self-pity blinds the eyes so that we fail to recognize the signs from Him that say, "I am caring for you. I am with you in this."

Climate is relatively unimportant if you have a job indoors or in a city office with an air conditioner, or can ride to work in a pleasantly insulated car. Missionary trekking takes you outdoors in all weathers and often, still, on your own two feet — and then it does seem to matter. "But surely," you say, "missionaries should live above such trifles as weather." It would be nice to be able to say we are so taken up with our missionary task that we don't notice if it is hot or cold, but it would not be true. We drip perspiration, our clothes cling to us uncomfortably, and we sometimes feel as if it takes too much effort to do anything more strenuous than breathe. Others thrive on the heat but have sniffles all through the rain. In any case we all need the Lord's grace to "weather the weather." He is able to be a cloud that shelters from the heat, to refresh us when we are parched and dry, and to send breezes in answer to prayer.

When I fussed about the rain or wished it were cooler I would quote to myself Amy Carmichael's poem, which is really about something more important than weather:

"We do not ask to choose our garden's
 weather,
 Too ignorant are we.
 Only that we, Thy gardeners together,
 May pleasure Thee."

This helped if I allowed it to. Sometimes I preferred to fuss.

Chapter 5

We Wish You A Happy Fright

ONE OF PEOPLE'S first impressions of Thailand's capital is the traffic. It is hair-raising. A newspaper article once wryly pointed out that an invading army crossing the Thai border would find no difficult terrain to hinder its advance, till it encountered Bangkok traffic. I have spent considerable time at the edge of Bangkok streets trying to summon the courage to dart across between the hurtling vehicles. The best plan is to wait until a small group wants to go across together, and hope that the traffic will obey the English injunction, painted in the road at busy corners, "beware of the pedestrians." One day I stood so long on a street corner that a little old Chinese granny came to my rescue. Holding up a commanding arm to stop the traffic she took me by the hand and led me safely across.

We early learned to pray about safety in travel. "For He has charged His angels to guard you wherever you go," said the Psalmist. This keeps the angels fully occupied. Someone should add up the total number of missionary kilometers trudged on foot in Thailand, the hours spent compressed in small buses, the miles covered on bikes and motor bikes. It would be an impressive total, and all under the watchful care of His messengers. We also learned to avoid the front seats of buses, for if you don't know your bus is passing another bus on the brow of a hill, you enjoy the trip more.

Better roads, and more of them, have changed the picture considerably since the days when we perched precariously on top of rice sacks in an open truck or wedged in amongst barrels of petrol, pigs, provisions and people in an open-sided bus. Between the main cities there are now comfortable tour buses, with reclining seats and air conditioning, with Pepsi and snacks served by a charming Thai hostess. Missionaries no longer spend nights in the jungle en route to their tribal homes. Farmers still use oxcarts for farm work especially in rice harvest, but I am glad they are no longer public conveyances. I have vivid memories of "enjoying" these contraptions.

Once when moving to a Lahu Christian village we traveled with a "caravan" of oxcarts. The drivers would not let the family go in one oxcart, saying it would be too heavy, so Larry and baby Gordon went in one, preschoolers Marilyn and Shirley with me in another, and our stuff was spread around the rest. In spite of the weight problem, sacks of cement, baskets of coconuts and bags of rice were taken on along the way, and as they kept adding more and more cement my initial irritation gave way to amusement! Being in two carts while lunch was packed for one meant Larry doing a lot of running back and forth, holding Gordon in one hand and raisins and hard-boiled eggs in the other. It was impossible to relax in a two-wheeled cart with no springs. We felt every bump; the road was wet and often boggy and we lurched into deep holes. At one point four other cart drivers hung onto the side of our cart to prevent it turning right over. I had seen another missionary mother and her small daughter turn over into a filthy bog on that very road so I knew it was possible.

While we lived beside the Mekhong river, boat travel was the only possible way of getting near the trail to the Lahu villages. One Sunday we had hurried down to the boat landing to catch the 6.30 a.m. boat upriver. It was already occupied by a Thai family, some Lao women with bulging bamboo market baskets, a few upriver Chinese and some school boys. The seats, being six inches wide and six inches off the floor, were never planned for long-limbed foreigners with a tendency to backache, but that was all there was so we sat for an hour until the boat took off. Only a few hundred yards up the river we pulled in to a low beach strewn with household effects. A family was moving house on our boat! The next hour was whiled away watching mattresses, kettles, chickens, cardboard boxes, nets and carrying poles being stowed away wherever a spot could be found. Finally Father appeared carrying two small children, and we were off.

The monsoons hadn't yet come and the Mekhong was low, revealing rock masses that I hadn't known were there. Suddenly there was a grinding sound; the boat shuddered, the pilot shouted and shut off the engine. The rudder had been knocked off by a hidden rock. We drifted while various ineffectual remedies were applied, but finally there was nothing for it but to drift to a nearby island where we waded ashore, found a small dugout canoe to cross an unwadeable channel, and walked to the nearest ferry to find another boat. When we reached our village at 1.30 p.m. we found our Lahu congregation had long since finished their 11 o'clock meeting. But they sympathized with us over a seven-hour trip that could have been done in three, and sat down to have another service with us.

From one Lahu village we had to walk out through the forest and stand on the river bank, frantically waving umbrellas and handkerchiefs to attract the attention of passing boats. Sometimes they saw us and sometimes they didn't. So much of travel is not traveling, but waiting. How did we spend the time? Sometimes there were opportunities to witness, or at least give out some tracts. Books and the Word helped. I learned to carry paper and pen and many of my friends received letters, thanks to an uncertain transport schedule. Better missionaries than I would, no doubt, have spent the time in prayer. Sometimes I could do this but often my prayers were frantic appeals to the Lord to speed a boat or a car to us. I could empathize with a skit acted at one of our mission parties, in which a girl was supposed to be sitting by the road waiting for a bus. There were impatient gestures, biting of nails and frequent glances at her watch. Finally she said: "I'd better pray," and as she reverently bowed her head and closed her eyes, the bus whipped past! At times during those long waits I felt bored and restless and then my prayer was to endure happily. Through it all the Lord wrought in us a degree of patience, which is not to be despised.

Away from the main roads we still travel in small public *song taos*, which are really baby buses about the size of a pickup truck. The Thai name means "two rows", narrow seats along the sides behind the cab. Depending on the size of the *song tao* each side comfortably seats five to eight people, but any respectable driver fills it uncomfortably full. Our son Alan, on a trip to a Hmong village, said on his return: "I learned something this trip. 39 people can travel on one *song tao*." They sit on the roof and hang on the sides and back, and those inside, along with the baggage at their feet, are wedged in so tightly they can't even wiggle.

The Thai are generally petite and slim and the larger buses are built for their proportions. This means that missionaries must have telescopic or collapsible knees, for there are times when you must fit a 24-inch hip-to-knee measurement into 20 inches of space. Or you may measure 18 inches across and find that your allotted share of the seat is 9 inches. A missionary must be adaptable.

Wheeled vehicles can take you only where there are roads, and tribal villages, especially mountain ones, are generally off the beaten track. Then your own feet are the only mode of transport. You travel in single file, and the privileged position is in the middle. The person in the lead breaks the spider's webs, shakes the dew off the grasses and gets to face the dogs when you go into a village. The third party has them at his heels. There is no position of privilege in regard to leeches, which are at the height of vigor in the rainy season when the path is likely to be overgrown and bushes brush you as you pass. As new missionaries we were told you could cut them off with a knife, and there was an interesting observation about leeches not liking salt. But how many missionaries travel with salt and knife in hand? We found the quickest method was to smother them in a leaf and then they would let go.

Trekking also poses the problem of how to protect yourself from the rain. Inside a raincoat you would perspire so much that its purpose of keeping you dry would be thwarted. A lot of folk use big sheets of plastic which can be draped over head, shoulders and backpack and still give you space to breathe. I myself belong to the umbrella school of thought. This has the disadvantage of leaving only one hand for other things, but I am practically blind without my glasses so an umbrella seems imperative. It does make you lopsided on the trail, though, when there are sharp rocks to climb over or fallen trees to impede your progress. Keeping your balance on the descent is not easy. It is here that you collect your badges of mission-ary service — discolored toe nails, or even no toe nails at all. I often wished I had four hands to keep

me upright on the path, but my husband nobly
loaned me one of his and that helped. He towed
me up many a mountain, and when the brakes in
my legs were gone, he prevented me from falling
down into the abyss. If you don't have a husband
you must make it on your own.

Some of the best lady missionaries disdain
umbrellas even for the sun. They use broad-
brimmed hats, generally the useful not orna-
mental variety. It has now become acceptable
in Thailand for ladies to wear slacks for traveling
and this facilitates mountain climbing. It can also
lead to confusion. Let me introduce you to the two
Barbaras. Barbara Good and Barbara Hey, both
from New Zealand, work together amongst the
Blue Hmong, and as their signatures read
"B. Good" and "B. Hey" they are popularly
known as "Be good" and "Behave." Near the top
of a faraway mountain the two not-yet-middle-
aged Barbaras and some Hmong friends met a
group of Hmong people who probably had not
seen foreigners before. One lady in the party
gazed wonderingly at them and asked: "Who are
these two old Chinese grandfathers?"

I have said nothing so far about stream cross-
ings, about forty of them on the way to one
Hmong village. You can't stop forty times to take
off your shoes and socks, so you wade in shoes and
all. En route to one of our Lahu villages the
stream was the trail. I haven't mentioned bridges
that are one solitary slippery log, which make
even the stoutest heart quail. And I have omitted

the delicate art of balancing on the narrow dikes that edge the rice fields. Yes, travel can be demanding.

What's the purpose of it all? There are people God cares about at the end of the road, and along the road for that matter. God has something wonderful to be shared, something they won't know unless a traveler gets out on the trail to tell them. The joy of the message to be shared is a moving force, and the sense of God's presence as you go is an enveloping reality. The greatest joy comes when the message is received, but this joy rarely, if ever, comes at the first visit. It is hard for us to picture people who know nothing of the Scriptures. In our near-pagan societies in the West very few have true faith in Jesus Christ, but most know who you mean when you refer to Him. They have some foundations upon which to build. Our tribal friends have none, and it takes time to lay a foundation.

There are days when you feel tired or when a cloud is waiting to burst upon you, days when you do not want to go and visit another village. You know it is a privilege but it doesn't "feel" like one. Then you move in sheer obedience, and then it is a help to know that there are people at home who are sharing in the toil in prayer.

During our time in Laos a twenty-minute plane ride into a remote mountain area could save us three days of stiff walking. A caretaker at the small airstrip would chase off the grazing water buffalo before the plane landed, and from there in a matter of hours we would climb to find the Lahu folk who needed to hear God's good news. But those twenty minutes in the plane were terror filled. For at least two days before each trip I was physically ill with apprehension. It wasn't so much the thought of crashing, as panic at being enclosed in a small Cessna Wren so many yards off the ground. Cornelia Otis Skinner tells how in the early days of flight travel when passengers were invited to visit the cockpit she felt compelled to stay in her seat, to listen to the engine, to watch for emergency landing fields, and to balance the plane. I know exactly what she means. I was too scared to watch for landing fields but I did feel the necessity of balancing the plane and this was an exhausting procedure. I prayed about it, and other people prayed for me, but it didn't seem to help. I quoted Scripture to myself but I was still terrified. Then one day I said: "Lord, I am at the end of myself. I can't endure the pre-flight dread and the actual flying any longer. I cannot face another trip unless you deliver me from this paralyzing fear." God did answer that prayer. He did not remove *all* the fear, but He gave peace. I still didn't look forward to the flights but my stomach behaved beforehand, and although I never enjoyed them I wasn't nervously exhausted by them anymore.

Once on an Asian airline the pilot who spoke on the intercom welcoming passengers aboard was having trouble with his pronunciation. The wish that he expressed was that we might all have a "happy fright." This felicitous phrase describes my state of mind while in the air; happy and frightened, uneasy yet assured, a sense that God is present and in control, plus the feeling that I will be glad when it is over. I was grateful for that deliverance in Laos but often felt guilty that it seemed only partial. The psalmist said God delivered him from *all* his fears, but He had not done this for me. Was I at fault? I still don't know the answer but it was a comfort to notice that David also said: "What time I am afraid, I will trust," which suggests that the emotion of fear can exist side by side with faith. The books all tell us that fear and faith are mutually exclusive, but I am now persuaded that even when my knees knock I can still trust the Lord.

Fellow missionary Leona Bair asked me to go with her to visit some Hmong villages, and as we sat on the bus I vividly remembered childhood visits with my father to three different churches on Sundays. Those Saskatchewan roads were innocent of gravel or paving and I can still feel my childish terror as the rain poured down and the car slithered along, almost out of control. The familiar reaction swept over me that day in the bus on a muddy unpaved road, while Leona sat comfortably beside me, composed and blasé. Finally we got back to paved road and I leaned back with relief, but now it was Leona's turn to sit on the edge of her seat and bite a few nails. For she worries about the driver going to sleep. She buses many uncomfortable hours praying that the driver will stay awake until they reach the place where she can get out and walk.

Eileen Guder says: "Life can be truly exciting when we are really free of crippling fears. Most of us have hardly begun to grasp the magnitude of the freedom that can be ours. We think being free of fear means being safe and protected, that there is no need for anxiety; but that's really not freedom at all. To live like that is to be in bondage to whatever circumstances we need to have to feel safe. Real freedom from fear is present even when we are in the midst of dangerous situations, or confronted with sudden disaster. It frees us from the slow wearing poison of constant anxiety and apprehension; and it enables us to do and be what God really intended for us."[1]

To be delivered from *all* fear is one of God's miracles, and it would make traveling nicer and more comfortable. But surely it is also one of God's miracles that keeps Leona on the buses. His deliverance from fear frees us to travel wherever He wants us to go, even with bus drivers who look as if they need to nap.

I love Bishop Houghton's poem that says:
"Not trembling we go, afraid,
   Not fearful, hesitant, dismayed,
   But firmly on our Refuge stayed
   We go."

Many of us cannot say the first two lines of the poem with honesty. We do tremble and hesitate, but we can go on once again because we know our Refuge.

---

[1]*Deliver us from fear*

"We know the Rock whereon we stand.
We know a strong unfailing Hand.
We know a Heart that our life planned.
We know."

God has to give us courage to travel; He also has to give wives the courage to free our husbands to travel. When a missionary wife waves her husband off on a preaching trip she is likely to be asking herself, "What will happen to him?" and "What will happen to me?" These are not silly questions, for many things can happen to either of them. Hundreds of treks have been completed without any mishap, but from some missionary journeys the husband never returned. It seems almost impossible not to be anxious if he is delayed, and the imagination can run riot. I know of only one remedy — large and frequent doses of the Word.

Amy Carmichael writes:

"I see Thee guide the frail, the fading moon
    That walks alone through empty skies at
        noon;
    Was ever way-worn lonely traveler
    But had Thee by him, blessed Comforter?"[2]

We tend to think that God's promises are only for those who pioneer and dare great deeds for His sake. But the staying-at-home-to-look-after-the-children mother can also be way-worn and lonely, and for her too He has promised His presence "even unto the ends of the earth."

---

[2]*Wings*

Chapter 6

Our Daily Bread

ONE WEEK LARRY and I were host and hostess to a group of Canadians, and on their first evening we took them out to eat at a nice Thai café. We had ordered food in advance, specially choosing dishes that would be bland and mild enough for a foreign palate, and asking that only a little pepper be put in. Everything was beautifully prepared in the rustic open air restaurant, and our visitors enjoyed sampling the food. But sampling was all they could manage. They consumed gallons of cold water to soothe their burning mouths! At that point I decided I should have told the cook not to put *any* peppers in, and then the amount she would have felt compelled to put would have been just right for our foreign friends.

Before I went to China I thought I was facing a lifetime of rice pudding! I dislike all puddings and rice pudding, even with raisins, heads the list of "foods I can do without," so I was considerably relieved when I discovered that the Chinese hardly ever eat pudding. Rice was, however, our staple diet, and who could object to it served with tasty Chinese-style vegetables and meat. It is equally good with Thai food. Thai curries! With meat simmered in coconut milk, and spices and peppers! I confess to wanting to limit the number of tiny green peppers put in the curries, however.

A Thai cook given the freedom of the kitchen can make curries hot enough to put a permanent curl in your hair.

All the missionary children I know love rice. I remember one little boy whose supreme delight was plain rice plentifully sprinkled with *nam pla*, the Thai liquid equivalent of salt. And they all love the Northern Thai favorite, sticky rice eaten with the fingers, dipped into sauces with meat, flavored vegetables and barbecued pork sticks. When our Alan chose the menu for his birthday meal, he chose sticky rice.

A quick visit to the Chiang Mai fresh food market would convince you of the wide variety of food available. The market proper is made of brick but along its sides and at the back beside the river there are open air stalls where people sit beside their baskets to display their wares. Through its two lanes small trucks and *song taos* may pass, causing traffic snarls and possible danger to limb but, as all vehicles proceed at caterpillar speed, not to life. You spend a lot of time waiting for them to pass, while your arms are stretched out of their sockets with hanging on to all your market bags. I did the shopping for Pinecrest, our mission's holiday cottage on a nearby mountain, so I often engaged in this arm-lengthening exercise. The real danger lies with the two-wheeled market trolleys, or rather their drivers. When a normally polite Thai person pushes one of these carts, something happens to him. He believes he should have the right of way, so he jostles and pushes and shouts at the innocent marketers.

According to the season, you may find stalls of delicious fruit such as mangoes, mangosteens, rambutans, *lamut*, pineapples, *lum yai* and jack fruit. Papayas are full of vitamins and are delicious sprinkled with lime juice. And durian — you either love it or loathe it, there is no in between. You can buy bananas — long, short or fat. There are twenty varieties altogether. There are all the usual vegetables, even potatoes and carrots because the tribal people grow these in the hills. In other parts of Thailand, potatoes are expensive and usually only bought for a treat. And then there are things like bean sprouts and mushrooms, the peas that you eat shell and all, and Chinese cabbage.

But this is Chiang Mai. The smaller markets have food, of course, but offer much less variety. And in the tribal villages there are usually no markets at all. So most of our missionaries must make periodic visits either to the Chiang Mai or Chiang Rai centers in order to replenish their food supplies.

The great problem is meat. Some folk fry it and keep it salted and covered with fat. Tinned meat is too expensive to buy. Some meat can be frozen solid ahead of time, and if wrapped well in newspaper will hopefully reach home without spoiling. It is a grim business buying a two to three week food supply to take to a tribal village. The food must survive a long trip in the heat, and even if there is a refrigerator at home it can't contain it all. First you buy it all and lug it to the Mission Home in town. Then you must pack it, especially the eggs, well enough to survive a bumpy trip. The Mission Home living room is quite often an untidy conglomeration of cardboard boxes, old newspaper, cabbages and onions, while two or three folk pack up for leaving next morning. Then all the stuff has to be put on a local bus. Some people have to get off the bus at some point and transfer it all to a *song tao* and perhaps even carry it the last quarter mile into the village. If there is no major road to your home then you have the bother of arranging for carriers, and loads must be packed with the proper weights for either people or horses.

One solution to the fresh food problem is to have your own garden, but you must keep your morale at a high level to cope with the gardening trials. First, you must have a fence strong enough to keep out the neighbor's pigs. Unless you have had some acquaintance with tribal pigs you will have no idea of the strength required. Second, you must be willing to chase out the neighbor's chickens. Third, you must carry buckets of water from the nearest source, usually some yards away. Fourth, you must be willing to harden your heart against everyone who wants to share the things in your garden. Fifth, you must be able to forgive the people who sneak in and help themselves. And sixth, you must be vigilant against snails. After you have battled your way through all these problems you may feel it is too much fuss and abandon your agricultural leanings.

The local people do share their garden produce. When we lived in Lahu villages we were overwhelmed with cucumbers. These were not picked when they were young and tender — that wouldn't be good value for your money — but allowed to grow to a huge size, at least a foot in length, and were an orangey color inside. We ate them raw in salads, cooked with onions, cooked with meat or tomatoes. And then we would start over again on our cycle. If I had had any imagination I should have been able to produce a cucumber pudding! By the end of the cucumber season I hated the sight of them! We couldn't possibly eat all that were given to us, and I confess that more than once we dumped cucumbers in the jungle or surreptitiously put them out for the ever-present free-roaming pigs.

In the good old days, parents insisted on their children eating everything on their plates. That kind of upbringing is good preparation for the mission field. At my first glimpse of a certain Lahu delicacy, I thought it was a sunflower with particularly large seeds. But when the "seeds" moved, I took a second look and realized it was bee larvae. This was such a treat to the Lahu, and we had to appreciate their desire to share it with us. I told myself that food likes and dislikes are purely a matter of getting used to them. The Lahu think that our cheese smells so bad and tastes so horrible that no civilized person would eat it. So I would accept the small wrigglers and keep them in a cupboard so that, if anyone should ask me how I liked them, I could say we hadn't eaten them yet. When I was sure no questions would be asked, I could throw them out.

If you are trekking and witnessing in tribal villages, or if you live in one, you are likely to be introduced to life's more exotic foods. On one of Larry's excursions he was fed venison, jungle fowl, porcupine, fish and partially incubated eggs. Monkey meat and tree fungus we rather liked. Even if you don't care for sweet potatoes, they are delicious when they come steamy hot from the coals of a Lahu fire. You don't even want butter and salt.

We operated on the principle that we could eat whatever was put in front of us, and generally that principle caused no great strain. Once we were in a village at New Year's time when there were special festivities and food. People were always at home then so it was a good time for witness. A pig had been killed for the occasion and we watched the meat being chopped very fine, flavored with chopped tree bark and rolled into balls. These were tossed into hot fat for one minute, no longer, and served with our breakfast rice. We had misgivings about those meatballs, for there was no way they could have been cooked through, but true to our principle we ate them and they were delicious. We left immediately after eating, because we had several hours walk ahead of us, down the mountain to the small village on the plain where we hoped we might catch a plane out to our home. There was no plane schedule; you just sat by the airstrip until one appeared. Our longest wait was six days, but it was usually one or two. After a while I began to feel uneasy and by the time we got to that small village on the plain I didn't care if there was a plane or not. We went to the small bamboo house we rented there, as a base for going into the mountains, and I collapsed and was gloriously ill.

When you get the food to your village you must further complicate life with cooking. If charcoal is easy to get you can use a charcoal stove, which looks like a flower pot with a grate for the ashes to fall through. A small tin oven can sit on top of it, albeit rather precariously. One day when I was baking, the oven fell off the stove and out through an open window, crashing to the ground below. The fall broke the glass in the oven door, but didn't hurt the cake which was nearly done anyway. Larry promptly fixed up a stand to keep the oven in its place. A few missionaries have an open fire on the floor, complete with tripod, black sooty kettles and ricepots. It is amazing what good food can come out of an oven on a open fire, but unless your wood is well seasoned you are kept busy tending the flame. The fire is the center of social activity, for folk sit around it and talk. It also keeps the house well smoked. In fact, you can usually tell the missionaries who have an indoor fire, for when they first arrive at the Mission Home their clothes tend to have a well-smoked, well-cured scent!

When I lived in a tribal village I was dismayed at the amount of time I spent preparing food. There are no short cuts. There is no running to the corner store for frozen foods — there aren't any — or tinned food — too expensive. There isn't even a store. If you want rice krispies for breakfast, you dry rice in the sun and puff it in the frying pan. If you want peanut butter you must grind the peanuts in the meat grinder. If you like bread you must be prepared to bake, beginning the process by sieving the flour to get rid of the baby weevils (brown) and the adult weevils (black). Good food can come from weevily flour, but when it reaches the stage that even a veteran missionary cannot eat what is made from it, it must be thrown out and you either make another long trip to town or go without bread. The effort to keep food from spoiling amounts to battle proportions. In the intense heat cooked food goes off very quickly, and in the humidity the bread soon sprouts mould.

We always had enough food in our tribal homes, but the lack of variety was a problem. When my husband and two Lahu companions were evangelizing in Lahu villages, they had rice and mustard greens for breakfast, lunch and supper — for seventeen consecutive meals! The tender mustard plant is delicious but the flavor palls after the first six times. Rice three times a day is too boring for most westerners and we tried to have a few changes like our foreign breakfast, or noodles or macaroni for supper. I found that an ancient Boston school cookery book fitted our lifestyle better than the modern type that starts out "take two tins of mushroom soup." If we had two tins of mushroom soup in the hills we would serve them as soup, not put them in something! Or the recipe begins with an impossibility like "put the following ingredients in the blender." What? No blender? No electricity! It is not easy to be a creative cook when you must, perforce, resort to the same old thing for supper. On the other hand you don't need to spend a lot of time planning menus. So you eat what you have and are thankful.

Are you saying to yourself that missionaries ought to be thinking of higher things than food? We don't spend our entire energies on it, but it does matter. The Lord Himself said we might pray for our daily bread. So it is not wrong for a mother to be praying for nourishing food for her children, or even for some special treats for a birthday celebration. Galery Panov, a Russian ballet dancer who suffered greatly as a Jew trying to escape from Russia, said of the days of persecution and privation: "It sounded noble to be fighting for our principles, but the dreary truth was that we were spending as much time thinking about our stomachs." The rightness of his cause did not prevent hunger pains. And so it is with us. We all have our moments when we think longingly of McIntosh red apples (Canadian variety — the best in the world), or Swiss cheese, or whatever our favorite national dish happens to be. Our calling as the servants of the Lord does not subtract from our humanity.

Mountain rice has much more flavor than the rice grown on the plains, and more food value too, for it is handmilled and retains the bran that covers the kernel. Until about 1900 most rice in Thailand was milled by pestle and mortar, which is slow hard work. Commercial mills do a quick job but remove all the bran, which goes into the feed to keep the pigs and chickens fat and flourishing. It is no coincidence that beri-beri, caused by a vitamin deficiency, was not common in Thailand before 1900. Tribal people are now beginning to get power mills and this will mean a loss of nutrition that they can ill afford, for they do not get much protein. When hunting is good they have a feast, but the days of good hunting are nearly over. Most people raise some pigs and chickens but they are not normally used for a daily food source.

I remember some Yao complaining that they had nothing to eat. What were they talking about? Their gardens were overflowing with pumpkins and squash! But to them vegetables are not really food, only accompaniments to go with their rice. They regard vegetables as we regard pickles, and no one wants to live exclusively on condiments. Vegetables and bits of meat merely provide flavor for their rice. One of our Lahu hosts made out of one solitary egg a dish to supplement rice for seven people. It was like a tasty soup with bits of egg floating in it, and just helped our food to go down.

When the rice harvest is poor, the tribes really suffer. On one trip the new rice crop was not ready to harvest so the Hmong were using dried corn as a substitute. It was stone ground mixed with water, and cooked. Being tasteless and saltless, it went round and round in my mouth and resisted swallowing. It was ghastly stuff. But that's all they had, and they shared it with us. The tribal people are always hospitable, even when they have little food for themselves. If you happen to be a special guest of the Hmong you are feasted frequently. Larry was accompanying one of the Hmong missionaries, and in one village they were awakened about 3.30 a.m. as the two girls of the household started the fire, put on rice, killed and prepared a chicken. They ate a delicious meal at about six. Just after they finished, another lady came to invite them to her house for breakfast, where they sat down to rice and fat pork. The Hmong say: "If you cannot smile, at least show your teeth; if you cannot eat at least hold a spoon." That was about all they could do when yet another Christian invited them to a meal of rice and wild boar meat. They felt truly fortified by the time they left at seven for their homeward journey!

In Thailand the "staff of life" is rice, not bread. They may use slices of bread to wrap around ice cream, or to dip, toasted, into sweetened condensed milk for breakfast. But rice is the mainstay. If tribal people know what bread is, they regard it as a foreign snack, so Jesus' statement "I am the bread of life," has little meaning. A meaningful paraphrase would say: "Jesus is the rice of life." Without rice they know they cannot live. Tribal churches usually use rice in the Lord's supper and this has its own symbolism, for the rice must fall into the ground and die before new life is possible.

How many ways God has of teaching us, tribal Christians and missionaries alike! He can take the simplest elements of life to remind us that He is essential to our growth, that He feeds and sustains us. It is when I am at my weakest that I fully appreciate that He is the source of my energy and strength. "I carry Thee on my journey, O Son of God. And my hunger is stayed by Thee, O Savior of the world."

Chapter 7

He Came To Mend Earth's Broken Things

A MIDDLE-AGED Lahu lady named Na-U would often come to us for pills. She had what appeared to be an abdominal tumor, and we tried to persuade her to go to a doctor but she wouldn't listen. One day she sent one of her children over with a request for medicine. At first I refused; then my conscience smote me and I sent some aspirin to tide her over. Later in the day we noticed a flurry of excitement at Na-U's. The village idlers and the children went running to her house, and someone hurried to the woodpile and carried in a load of wood. That night when folk gathered in our house for their evening visit, I enquired after Na-U. "Oh, she's fine," someone said, "and the baby is doing fine too."

Neither my husband nor I have had any medical training. Not wanting to be well-meaning missionaries who, through ignorance, did a lot of harm, we had thought we wouldn't do any medical work. But you can't sit beside a bleeding child and say you aren't trained to do medical work. Qualified or not, we did medical work. Sometimes it consisted of aspirin and prayer. One young stalwart fell and tore open his chest on a bamboo stump. Bamboo is highly infectious and I was afraid we couldn't handle it, but antibiotics and clean dressings brought healing.

One day a young Lahu man from a distant village came to our home. He had fallen into the fire in an epileptic fit, and the odor from the wounds on his horribly burned body was so bad that we kept him out on the porch. I was so grateful that a trained nurse was visiting that day, for when the cloth covering his wound was removed, the flesh was full of maggots. She did what she could, and then we pleaded with him to go to the hospital. He refused, as they so often do. The wounds eventually healed, but the muscles in his arm contracted and he will go through life with an almost useless right arm.

Na Gu, having her first baby, had been in labor for five days. Her family kept hoping things would right themselves, but finally they decided to take her to hospital. They had waited too long, and she died on the trail. She was just a child herself, but we believe she was God's child too.

There are several reasons for the tribal folks' reluctance to go to the town for medical help. First there is the expense, and then the distrust of people outside their own area. They realize they are unpopular with the Thai, and they are not fluent in the Thai language. Hospitals and their bewildering procedures frighten them. One of our missionaries brought an almost blind Akha man to the eye specialist in the Chiang Mai hospital. He had to go through the routine procedure to enter as a patient, and was thoroughly mystified by the taking of his temperature and the urinalysis. What did any of this have to do with his bad eye?

Although there are many fine doctors in Thailand, there are also a lot of "quacks" who travel in the mountains giving injections to anyone in the mood for a shot. People want injections and feel as if they haven't had proper treatment unless a needle is inserted somewhere. Beate Kaupp, who worked amongst the Pwo Karen, found her medical skills were often needed. When she was treating a Karen woman who was hemorrhaging dangerously, the woman was annoyed that Beate would not give her an injection. She took the pills specified, but because they didn't take effect instantaneously she went off to a "quack" and for a princely sum was given an injection. Of course this did not help and Beate and her fellow missionary, Christa Weber, finally had to take the patient to the Chiang Mai hospital. The treatment was successful, but when Beate and Christa went to take her home to her village, she was still complaining and unhappy, because the hospital staff hadn't given her an injection either! They tried to point out the important thing was that she was healed, but she wouldn't be mollified. She felt cheated of proper care.

This love of injections is not shared by missionary kids who, in addition to the ordinary ones children get at home, have to have cholera, typhoid and typhus as well. Four-year-old Jane was being led by her mother into a mission hospital gate. When Jane saw where they were going, she said: "Oh, let's not go in here. This is dangerous!"

A young Lahu man wanted us to sell him two antibiotic pills. Knowing that to take such pills frequently for minor ailments reduces their effectiveness in a dangerous illness, we refused. He was upset and said we didn't care about him. Didn't we know how quickly the Lahu can die from even a trifling illness? This kind of pressure is hard to bear, and they can make a nurse feel almost guilty for refusing to give an injection. Seeing that otherwise they are likely to go to a "quack" and get something that may do them harm, some nurses have solved the problem by giving Vitamin B shots, for the people that come are always undernourished or weak from long-standing sickness.

Someone overheard a conversation between two traveling "doctors." One was extolling the merits of penicillin and told of cures he had seen. Then the other man shared his new medical discovery. "I have found a good way to make medicine act quickly," he said solemnly. "I first give an injection of sweetened condensed milk, and that makes medicine flow quickly through the body." Even our untutored medical help was an improvement on this.

But we did silly things too. A Lahu man from another village came asking for medicine and quoting symptoms that sounded like hepatitis. Our house was dark, so Larry led him out on the porch to examine his eyes. He looked normal and this was puzzling — until we found out that it was his brother that was ill! And a fellow missionary who shall be nameless managed to pull the wrong tooth out of a poor innocent's head.

It is true to say, however, that it was pills and injections that, in the mountains, opened the doors to the gospel. In the past, tribal people have had little reason to think that outsiders wished them well, so they were suspicious of the first missionaries and questioned their motive in coming. But you can make friends as you change dressings and dispense malaria pills. At one time Doe Jones, a nurse from Wales, was extremely busy attending to a village-wide epidemic of measles, and as a result the way opened into many homes formerly closed to her. Of course, Christians and non-Christians were treated and given the same cure. At first some of the new Christians thought that only Christians should be given help, but they came to see that medical aid is not a "reward" for believing, but is for anyone who needs it. There was one exception to this in the early days.

In Namkhet village, high in the mountains some two hundred miles south-east of Chiang Mai, the first Hmong had believed, turning from their spirit worship and saying they wanted to walk God's path. But the missionaries' joy over this was short lived, for a man named Fai Shoong came to the area and offered something better than the missionaries' stories. If the Christians would come with him, acknowledging him as leader, he promised them complete protection. No one would be ill, or die, and they would prosper financially. They must, of course, sever all ties with the Christian faith. These promises sounded too good to be true, but what if Fai Shoong really did have this power? It would be too foolish to miss such an opportunity. After talking it all over, six of the Christian families decided to accept, and the missionaries had to watch them leave the truth to follow a deceiver. They prayed, but there was no immediate answer.

At first it seemed as if Fai Shoong was right. Other families moved into his exclusive little settlement, and they did prosper. Their crops were abundant, their pigs fat and flourishing, and no one was sick. The first failure of his promise of protection occurred when one baby had a painful ear infection. I don't know what explanation Fai Shoong offered, but the mother was not interested in "explanations"; she wanted a well baby. Finally she went back to Namkhet and asked the missionary nurse, Doe Jones, for medicine.

The Christians in Namkhet were adamant that Doe was not to give any treatment of any kind. She was troubled, for she could only see an ailing child from whom she was withholding help. How could this be right? But the Hmong knew their own in a way the missionary could not, and they stood firm. If Fai Shoong had promised perfect health, then let him see to it. The unhappy mother realized the Christians were not going to relent and took her unhappy baby, her ear still streaming with pus, back home to Fai Shoong's village. She left an equally unhappy nurse who was not at all sure she should have listened to the Christians. Soon mother and suffering child were back on Doe's doorstep, but the Christians had not changed their minds. "No treatment or medicine for anyone from Fai Shoong's village." Again the mother carried her ailing baby back to Fai Shoong. And again Doe prayed over it, feeling torn between her nurse's instincts and the feeling that the Lord would never withhold help from anyone, deserving or otherwise; and the Christians' insistence that the sick baby was Fai Shoong's problem, not hers. The desperate mother finally persuaded two other families to leave Fai Shoong and become "Christians" again, so that the baby could have help. The child responded quickly to treatment.

When Fai Shoong's own son died, it was open proof that he had made promises he was powerless to keep. Those first believers from Namkhet left his village and truly submitted to the Lordship of Christ. One of the leaders in the Hmong church today lived in Fai Shoong's village as a boy. Fai Shoong himself died and Satan's attempt to delude came to nothing.

Peter and Dianne McIvor have experienced both the joy of giving medical help and the heartache of seeing it neglected. A Karen family from another village brought their three-year-old daughter to Dianne. The baby, a precious one for the first two children had died, had chronic diarrhea, was thin and looked ill. Dianne gave them antibiotics and a vitamin food preparation for babies, and strict instructions that the child was not to be allowed to eat corn, sugar cane or raw peppers. Later when she visited them she found the vitamin food had not been given to the child. The father said he didn't know how to prepare it, and because the child had cried for corn they had given it to her. A few weeks later the child was dead. It seemed so senseless.

Another family had two sick children. The boy took the medicine Dianne prescribed, and recovered, but the girl didn't like its taste. No one would force her to take it, so a week later she was gone. The family's reaction was, "Oh, she just wanted to die."

For a nurse to have a remedy in her hands but to be helpless to share it is emotionally wearing. And then there are baffling diseases with symptoms straying out of their proper places in the medical books. Nurses are called upon to do things that require the skill and training of a doctor. Two nurses had to set and plaster a broken leg. The Akha lassie was frantic with fleas that got inside the cast, and after standing it as long as she could she took it off. Fortunately the leg was nearly mended and finished healing on its own without the ministrations of the fleas. Another nurse had to sew back on a finger chopped off while cutting pig food. The responsibility is heavy. When patients die, there can be an aftermath of self-questioning: should I have given other medicine? Did I fail to make my instructions clear? The thousand and one accusing voices come from the one whose aim is to keep the child of God disturbed in heart. And, to top it all off, patients may include horses, and buffaloes, and pigs!

We non-medicals particularly welcomed the coming of competent doctors. When Dr. John Webb and his wife left their work in Burma and came to Thailand they were deluged with patients. But they recognized the danger of an over-full medical program, and he planned one dry season to bring the message of salvation to every village in the Khunyuam area (120 miles northwest of Chiang Mai). "There is a very great need for prayer support in the day by day work," he wrote once. "Without the constant supply of the grace of our Lord Jesus, the deep spiritual needs of the patients and their families go unnoticed, and the Word of the Lord does not reach them; time and energy are wasted on things which are done without the Lord's direction, and His business gets left undone."

All of us tried to stress the simple rules of health, like the virtues of plain soap and water. In most tribal groups one of the first efforts was a small book on hygiene. But it is not easy to keep clean in a tribal village. Some tribes do channel water into the village via split bamboo poles, but in many places the only source of water is yards away. It may be down a steep incline, slippery in the rainy season, with the water laboriously carried in bamboo tubes up to the homes. It is easier to go and bathe in the stream, which also serves as the village laundry. When I saw the difficulty of laundry I didn't blame Lahu mothers for having less-than-spotless children.

And then there is the matter of germs. The tribes believe all sickness comes from the "bite" of an evil spirit, and our talk about germs as small things you can't see that make you ill, just sounds like a foreign explanation of evil spirits. A Lahu friend who had TB used to stay with us when he came to town. After we discovered he was using Larry's toothbrush, I'm afraid we were cowards and removed the toothbrushes rather than explaining our germ theory. If a demon causes epidemics in a village, the only remedy the animist knows is to appease the demon with offerings. Careful washing of dishes and isolation of the sick does not make any sense to him. However, Christians who have turned from the old demon ways are becoming accustomed to the germ theory.

We missionaries have learned to boil our drinking water, especially important when our water supply was the river where people bathed and dumped their garbage. One small child came to her missionary mother in distress. "Mummy," she said sorrowfully, "I thought Deng really wanted to be a Christian, but she still drinks unboiled water!"

Getting people to follow instructions was another problem. The missionary would explain that one pill was to be taken each morning. "But surely," thinks the patient, "if one pill is good, two pills or even four would be more efficacious." There was always the worry that they would take too many pills, or not enough or, worse still, combine them with medicine bought from the local peddler. One day a Thai lad came to Doe asking for medicine for his granny. Doe explained most carefully the amount granny was to take, and the lad kept saying: "*Kap, Kap,*" meaning "Yes, I understand." Off he went with the pills, and when he was some distance down the road Doe realized she had been talking to him in Hmong! If she hadn't raced after him and told him all over again in Thai, he would have given granny her pills at his own discretion. Maybe he did anyway.

The tribal folk want instantaneous healing. If there is no improvement after one day, they assume the medicine isn't any good. Any long-term treatment is likely to be abandoned. Dr. Catharine Maddox asked Larry if he would take a Hmong couple to the Chiang Mai hospital. They traveled with him, stayed for a night in our tribal guest rooms, and next day were installed in the hospital where his wife was to have a month's cobalt treatment. She stayed exactly eight days, and then departed for home to do demon worship instead. When Dr. Catharine came to Chiang Mai at the end of the month she found that her patient had long since departed. You can't help but grieve over people who won't be helped, to say nothing of your wasted time and effort.

All of us, medicals and non-medicals, have felt our helplessness in the face of human need, but we have seen the Lord's intervention. He has used medicine and skillful care (non-skillful in our case!) in healing bodies. One teacher doing a nurse's job shared how the Lord had helped her in the treatment of two very sick Lisu children. Nor was it only missionary prayers that were answered. We rejoiced to hear A Byeh, a young Akha pastor, testify how the faith of newly believing families was strengthened through healings in answer to prayer.

"He came to mend earth's broken things,
　　That carpenter of old;
　God's broken law: man's broken hearts:
　　And broken dreams untold.

He came to mend earth's broken things,
　　To rest each weary soul,
　His body, broken on the cross —
　　Broken to make us whole."

Chapter 8

Wealthy Americans

IT WAS EARLY morning in the Laos mountains. The mists still lay heavy upon the plain below, but we were in the crisp clear air of a Lahu mountain village. We had flown in the day before to a small landing strip, and a two-hour climb had brought us to Ja Bee's village, miles from nowhere. Earlier that morning Larry had shaved in front of a fascinated audience, and was now out on the porch of our host's house, reading his Bible. A group of Lao traders passing through the village caught sight of a foreigner on the verandah, and one of the women darted over and asked Larry if he would put her son through college! We have often laughed over the episode, but it points up a perpetual problem. What financial aid should we give, and when, and where? What do we do about people's bodily needs?

For two and a half years we lived on the Laos side of the Mekhong River. To visit from the Thai side of the river meant clearing our way through a forest of red tape; it was easier to have a residence in Laos and we could then visit the Lahu in both countries. In this area of Laos were many refugees who had fled before the Communists. They had nothing, of course, and foreign agencies kept them alive. Even in tribal villages where no plane could possibly land, airdrops of rice and other necessities were a part of life. The children must have grown up thinking rice fell from heaven in plastic sacks! This all fostered the idea that foreigners had so much money they could throw it around.

The ideal plan was that the first year the refugees would be fed, the second year given seed and by the third year they were on their own. This was a sensible theory but it didn't always work, for handouts can cripple the will. A refugee mentality soon grows, bringing lack of self respect and effort and an undue dependence on the giver of largesse. We were besieged, in Laos, by people wanting money for funerals, for food, for sick relatives, for clothing or travel. We had no way of knowing if they truly needed help or not. It was terribly wearing. We hated saying "no", but we knew that there were people just waiting to take easy money from gullible foreigners.

The most obvious physical need in the tribal villages was for medical care. We were forced into dispensing medicine by the pressure of so many sick people, and we felt it was not in their best interests to give medicine without asking for payment. So we either charged cost price, or a nominal fee — just enough to allow the buyer to maintain his dignity. A young Hmong fellow spending some years in jail learned to read, did a correspondence course and found the Lord. So missionaries concerned about his re-entry into society arranged for him to spend a few months working at one of our mission hospitals. He had many aches and pains, but his free medical care didn't seem to help. On his first visit back to his tribal village he told his family that he wasn't well. "How much do you have to pay for your medicine?" was their first question, and when they heard it was free they said knowingly, "Of course free medicine can't help you. Go to the doctor and tell him you want medicine that you pay for." The doctor involved did not think this was as funny as we did!

It is true that people don't value what is free, so we charged something. In their early days amongst the Pwo Karen, Jim and Louise Morris lived in a village where anthropologists, wanting to gain the confidence of the people and feeling sorry for them, gave out free medicine. It was not easy for Jim and Louise to charge for their pills, and so to appear niggardly in contrast to the benevolent anthropologists. They too wanted the confidence of the people but they had the right principle and they stuck to it. It is not a principle that tribal folk always appreciate, however. Some don't want to pay and wonder why the rich missionaries are so stingy.

Karen women are usually adorned with multiple strings of beads, and literally cover their arms with bracelets. Louise once took a Karen lady to the hospital where the nurses insisted that, for cleanliness sake, all those bracelets had to come off. Some had not been removed for years so it was a traumatic experience for everybody. In an effort to help one of the Christians, Jim and Louise bought a supply of beads which he was to sell at a profit. This he did — but he was also to return the initial investment, which he did *not* do. Another Christian was given packets of brown sugar to sell and divide profits with the Karen who had supplied him, but he refused to turn over the original cost. In turn he gave another Karen bracelets to sell and that man wouldn't return the original cost. This breaks relationships, and the Morrises were forced to question if this kind of help really is a help.

We ourselves decided we would not lend money. If we felt it was needed we gave it outright. More often we gave food, or sometimes Larry would take the needy person to a cafe and see he was fed. We usually fed the Lahu at our house though they added considerably to my sense of inferiority — no matter how I poured chillies into the food they complained they couldn't eat much because it didn't taste like anything!

When we were in charge of the Mission Home in Chiang Mai some Hmong discovered that food as well as a tribal guest room was available for them. For a time we were besieged by Hmong — complete strangers walking in at any time of day asking for meals. We knew this was not Hmong custom, for a strict Hmong will not even ask for hospitality from a Hmong village unless someone from his own clan lives there. Larry had learned this the hard way when he was trekking in the mountains with a Hmong carrier. Around noon the carrier stopped near a Hmong village and, instead of going into the village for food as Larry expected, pulled out his own meal of rice. He explained to Larry that he had no clansman in that village so it would not be correct to go there for food. He hadn't told Larry to take any provision with him and he didn't offer to share his, so that day Larry climbed mountains on an empty stomach. Knowing this, I was hard put to it to feel hospitable to the groups of Hmong.

At last we asked Hmong Christians what we should do. They were horrified at the un-Hmong-like behavior. "Do *not* feed them," they advised. "Tell them they can use the tribal house but as you have no garden and no meat supply (which was certainly true) they will need to find a cafe and eat there." This was a relief for in addition to the inconvenience of providing food we didn't have on hand, I felt it was not good to encourage them to be beggars. We did provide a charcoal stove and things like fat and salt and matches so they could cook their own meals if they wanted to. So we had not abruptly refused them, but neither did we comply with undue demands.

On one occasion some Lahu women came to us in great distress. Their husbands had been more or less forced to join a local army and they were concerned as to how their children would be fed. Because they sounded on the verge of starvation, we loaded them with rice and also gave them money. A day or so later we happened to visit their village, and found that the children on the verge of starvation were chewing candy and sporting new toy watches. We couldn't see that our money had done much for the hungry.

A gift had been received to help Pwo Karen villagers, and as it was the cold season the missionaries decided to buy a good supply of blankets. Each family could buy one, paying a minimal amount so it would not seem like charity. But this ended up as a big headache, for some folk wangled it to get more than their share, while others complained bitterly that the blankets were too thin. Many of our attempts to help did not in fact help, for people just felt aggrieved because they didn't get as much as they wanted.

If we did refuse to give, I felt guilty and wondered about the verse that says, "Give to them that ask you." But I could see plainly that a handout to every Tom, Dick and Harry was not meeting the real need. Then I realized that this bothersome verse did not affect me when my children asked for things that were harmful. We said "no" to them then, though we did not enjoy the withholding.

One really successful attempt to improve the lot of the tribal people has been the skilled embroidery work done by the women. Tribal handicraft is big business these days. It started in a very small way with missionaries taking time to buy materials and then to market the beautifully fashioned dolls, purses, cushions and pictures. This was honest work for an honest price, and enormous help to Christians wanting to get away from growing opium.

Christians overseas were concerned for the Lisu believers. So at considerable cost and an inordinate amount of trouble some donkeys were brought to Bangkok by plane. A missionary then had to cut red tape and escort the donkeys up north. It was an interesting experience to say the least, and included having to bury one that died in Chiang Rai. Despite the cynical question, "Aren't there enough donkeys in the OMF without importing them from Australia?" cross breeding the donkeys with the small horses the tribal folk use has resulted in sturdy mules.

For some years, one of our missionaries has worked full time on helping the Akha with substitute crops. A friend from Switzerland brought some apple trees, which were doing well when in the missionary's absence one of his helpers had a burst of energy and pruned them so enthusiastically that they died. The bees also brought out from Switzerland swarmed off somewhere and could not be tempted back. As the suggested improvements depend on change of methods, the tribal folk have been slow to accept the new ways. Widespread change will likely come about only if and when neighbors see handsome cash returns.

Part of the guilt I felt in all this stemmed from the fact that we had so much more than the people around us. Right from the beginning we did try to eliminate non-essentials. But how do you define "essential"? In our early days in Thailand few

Thai homes had refrigerators. So should mission-aries have them or not? In that hot climate a refrigerator was not just a luxury, but a time saver and a health guard. Food will not keep overnight, which meant daily visits to the market at crack of dawn. Ellen, a friend from another mission, was anxious to live at the local level so did not have a refrigerator. But one day she heard the househelp chatting with a stranger on the front steps. The stranger was inquisitive and wanted to know all about Ellen and her belongings.

"Doesn't she have a fridge?" was the final question.

"Oh no," said the servant, "She is too stingy to buy one." It was a blow to Ellen who is *not* stingy. Knowing that going without a fridge was attributed to niggardliness, she got one.

We lived very simply in the Lahu villages, in an up-on-stilts house built for us by the Lahu with walls of split bamboo, and either a leaf roof or one of grass thatch. It is not as flimsy as it sounds because the leaves are huge; they overlap and are braided around thin bamboo withes. It is inconvenient in that they need renewing often, but they are much cooler than the corrugated tin roofs found more and more in Thai country areas, which are also deafening in a heavy downpour! When it wasn't raining I could see the occasional spot of blue sky where the leaves didn't quite meet, and would wonder what would happen in the next rain. The theory is that the leaves or grass swell with the damp, and this works more or less.

When it works "less" and your patching efforts are unsuccessful, you put your bed and your books in the driest places.

I rather liked the split bamboo floors, for the cracks let in any breezes and were useful for sweeping dirt through and for the neighbor kids to spit through. In letters home I must have sounded complaining about all the cracks and mosquitoes and other insects, for my mother wrote offering to screen our house for us. Bless her heart — with cracks in floor, roof and sides the only solution would be huge screen cages like a zoo!

Within the house we eliminated everything we could. In our bedroom we had mattresses on the floor, and a few cupboards made from packing boxes, one of which still showed the original wording "Guinness is good for you." It wasn't the thought we wanted to waken to first thing in the morning, but we never got around to putting on another coat of paint. Because the floor was so uneven it was hard to balance furniture, but we had a desk in the living room, a table and a few stools, plus one wicker arm chair which was a concession for our foreign backs. The Lahu sit on the floor and when we had guests we sat there too, but for me it was an ordeal. There were also more cupboards from boxes, and a few unframed pictures on the wall. No curtains. To us it looked bare and unhomelike, but not to our tribal friends.

It was our kitchen that gave the impression of boundless wealth. There was a clay-pot type of charcoal stove, a homemade table, and a screen cupboard whose legs stood in tins of water to keep out the ants. Box cupboards held our dishes. Our few pots and pans looked luxurious because they were not soot-blackened over a Lahu wood fire. Our small kerosene-operated fridge meant we had to have big tins of kerosene, and tin containers are an evidence of wealth. I tried to keep them as much out of sight as possible, but tins of flour and sugar seemed essential. Our boiled drinking water was poured into a baked clay container. There was a hand towel, and dish cloths and dishtowels, plastic bowls for washing dishes, and pails for water and garbage. We didn't have any more things around than the Lahu did — we had no strips of pork or peppers drying over an open fire, nor corn on a rack; no bows and arrows or guns hanging on the wall; no soot-covered kettle on a tripod, no fire for pigs' food, and no huge rice steamer. But our things looked so foreign, so different.

One thing we did have that was frankly foreign was a canvas swing that Gordon used to jump up and down in. Once when a band of robbers visited our village that swing disappeared, and later some of our villagers spied it hanging up in a nearby village. There was no mistaking it — it was the only canvas swing in Lahu land. So they nipped in and stole it back! I am afraid we did not scold them!

And then there was food. About once a week Larry would walk to the nearest market to bring back meat, fresh fruit and vegetables. I always hated unpacking it, for the Lahu would crowd round to see these incredible amounts of food. By our standards we ate very, very simply. Our noon meal was usually rice and a stew made out of what vegetable was available and a bit of meat. We branched out a little more for supper, but it was still simple. One time Larry developed a large boil on his neck and was really ill. The missionary doctor who "happened" to be visiting us said to me, "Your husband is not getting enough protein." I protested that we had so much more than the Lahu that we were ashamed to eat any better. "You just tell them I said the reason he is sick is because he hasn't had proper food," she insisted, so I told them. Whether they believed me or not I don't know. It wasn't easy to know the balance between having enough nourishing food to maintain our health, and knowing those around us didn't have the blessings we had.

A certain VIP was visiting some of our tribal stations, and we brought out some of our precious dainties for him, from our little store of treats sent in parcels from home and stored away for birthdays or guests. We were taken aback to hear later that he went home and announced that the North Thailand missionaries lived too well. We should have give him rice and peppers!

The whole matter of comparative standards of living and of material aid is a thorny one. We are moved by pity and give, and then discover that we have fostered a depend-upon-the-missionary-for-funds spirit. And this militates against the churches themselves learning to give to the Lord. Some people feel that tithing is legalistic, but God does honor it. All believers —poor and rich alike — need to grow in the grace of giving. Paul said of the Macedonian churches that "their deep poverty overflowed in the wealth of their liberality." J.O. Fraser would not give the first Lisu believers in China as much as a pencil, and he taught tithing right from the beginning. Niggardly? Blind to their physical needs? No. He had a clear vision of a completely self-supporting church, and the Lisu church has prospered.

I don't know all the answers; I can only record my own uneasy questionings, and my observation that many of the people who have received the most financial help are mercenary and spiritually poor. Some tribal believers today have bank accounts, a thing unheard of twenty years ago. They came to know God who set them free from bondage to the spirits with all its ineffectual sacrifices of pigs and chickens; they have prospered economically and I would not for a moment begrudge them the good things of life. But they are missing out on the things that God calls good. They have riches in the bank but care little about riches in Heaven, and this is reason for mourning.

We missionaries need help from the Lord in simplifying our life style so that people will feel at home in our homes. "Hospitality is the art of making people want to stay without interfering with their departure." Our charity should be a help, not a hindrance, and we need discernment to see the very fine line between the two. I am reminded of Augur's sensible prayer: "Give me neither poverty nor riches, but give me only my daily bread. Otherwise I might have too much and disown you and say 'Who is the Lord?' Or I may become poor and steal and so dishonor the name of my God."

Chapter 9

Don't Cry, Mummy!

"**I**-TUNG IS TEACHING Gordon to swear," complained our house girl one day. Five-year-old Gordon had picked up the Thai expressions that his friend I-tung used when he was cross, without knowing their meaning, and as my list of swear words was very small I hadn't known what Gordon was saying. I-tung presented us with other problems too. He set fires in our back yard, which could be terribly dangerous in the dry season. He smashed Gordon's new toy boat and said, when reprimanded, that Gordon gave him permission to smash it. Gordon probably did. When we caught I-tung stealing toys, he said our children gave them to him. And yet he was one of the most faithful members of our weekly children's meetings and we wanted him to hear more of the Gospel. We never saw any evidence that the Lord's word had touched his life, but who knows what was in his heart?

What effect does missionary life have on our children? Conscientious parents everywhere worry about the influence of other people's children, and having observed both oriental and occidental cultures I cannot see that the Canadian and American "heathen" are to be preferred to the Eastern ones.

It was difficult to know what to do about the

missing toys, however. We wanted our children to share, and didn't want to teach them to be grasping and hang tightly on to what was theirs. But we also wanted them to have toys to share! Unless they were suspicious and watchful everything would disappear. When Marilyn's beloved Teddy was taken, she was inconsolable. "Teddy will be missing me," she said, and so we prayed for Teddy's return, with little or no faith on the part of Marilyn's mother. Some time later a worse-for-wear Teddy was put back in the doorway of our front room. Maybe we didn't pray hard enough for the other things that were never returned.

Part of the problem of supervision can be solved by hiring a local girl as baby sitter. We were very happy with our Christian baby sitter Jan Dee, who cared lovingly for our first baby boy, and with her help I was able to get on with language study. However, we never could persuade her to say no to the demands of the older girls. If they asked for cookies they were given cookies, despite strict instructions that I alone was to be the dispenser of goodies. Observing other missionary children with their baby sitters we were not happy about their tactics for enforcing obedience, which might include threatening them with a crocodile or a demon. Alternatively, no attempt at all would be made to elicit obedience. We finally decided that an *amah* for the older children was not for us, and we managed to combine our work with child care.

By the time our youngest was at a roaming stage we were in a Christian tribal village, so small that he was never out of yelling distance. We let him go where he wanted, making periodic checks. He loved the Lahu and they loved him, and he was so royally fed that he didn't want much of what we set before him!

When we lived in Mission Homes, as we so often did, I was always self-conscious about disciplining the children before a long table full of guests. Should the peace and calm of pleasant dining be shattered while dealing with childish misdemeanors? Could we afford to let the cherubs go unrebuked? I am sure we made mistakes about this but we constantly prayed the parents' prayer, "Lord, give us wisdom." And we trusted that He had done so. The problem of discipline was even more pressing when the eyes of the locals were upon us. Most small children in the Orient are allowed to do what they want. Parents don't lay a hand on their offspring unless exasperation reaches such a peak that whipping is the safe release of tension. I have seen children being whipped with a switch, and lashed on the face, arms and bare legs by a mother almost crazed with anger; but this is unusual and would be frowned on as a complete loss of temper and face. A judicious whack or two on nature's intended spot is rarely known and would be interpreted as lack of self-control. One missionary traveling by train was gently burping her baby when a little old lady rebuked her, saying, "You should never hit a child!"

The locals never let a baby cry. They cannot understand feeding a baby on schedule, and think that only an unfeeling monster would allow a baby to cry in the night. Friends staying with us were having a rough night with their infant and finally, after feeding him and walking him for an hour or so, the mother put him down to cry it out. Very soon the neighbors were up, shining a flashlight into the bedroom and calling for the mother to awaken and tend to her child. They thought she was sleeping through the crisis and should be alerted! I used to fuss and fume over the night cries of our bairns. Should I spoil them by dashing to them at the first whimper, or let them cry and disturb the guests?

In spite of everything, we managed to have a lot of fun. Families ought to be building memories and this we were able to do. The happiest times in my sojourn in Thailand were when the three older children came home from their school in Malaysia for the twice yearly holidays. There was an exciting meeting at the Chiang Rai airport, a trip on a crowded bus, and then we took to the trail. In the rainy season this was horrendous, sloshing through mud that sometimes sucked off your shoes, wading streams, stopping for a picnic lunch along the way and again by the sulphur springs, and finally, when we were really weary after hours on the way, along the bamboo-shaded paths to Hweiyano village and home. This was simple in the extreme, but we belonged there and were part of the Lahu village family. They brought us cucumbers, new rice, mustard greens and corn on the cob. The children played games with the village children and competed with them at high jump and running. We did dishes together while someone read aloud from C.S Lewis's beloved Narnian tales. It was a very happy place to live.

Missionaries' children are likely to witness more of the realities of life than children at home, for tribal children are not spared the sight of suffering, and view the processes of birth and death. One small child came home and said casually, "I just saw a baby born." With our western desire for privacy and to shelter children from the nitty gritty of life, we have perhaps been overprotective. A Christian psychologist once told me that many missionary kids who come to him for counseling had suffered from too much parental protection on the mission field, rather than too little.

There are perils from which protection is needed, however. In tribal villages one of the most frightening perils is the unprotected log fire on the mud floor inside the house. If the house is on stilts, there is a built-in floor-level mud hearth. These fires are necessary for cooking, and for heat and light; and small children play right beside them. It is a marvel that more are not burnt. I have seen youngsters playing with burning sticks, but they seem to learn early to handle fire.

Houses on stilts usually have a verandah with no railing around it, and tribal babies must grow up aware of this hazard. We moved to a Lahu village when Gordon was a toddler, and that first day he frightened everybody with his mad dashes to the very edge of the verandah. On Monday morning a small group of Lahu men appeared with bamboo poles to erect a railing around the verandah, for Gordon's safety and their own peace of mind.

Gordon at three years old loved roaming the village, chasing the pigs and roosters. Some of the dogs, however, were dangerous, deliberately teased to make them bad-tempered watch-dogs. As long as neighbors were around they took pains to see that he was safe, but one day he climbed the steps to a Lahu house where no one was home. The dogs went for him, barking fiercely. He was frightened but stood his ground, waving a stick at them until someone came to his rescue. He then happily went on his way; but his cowardly mother dithered between fears for him and his need of some liberty. This, of course, is not a problem confined to the mission field. Anywhere in the world parents need to know how to teach a child about dangers that they may meet without teaching them to be unduly fearful. I didn't arrive at easy solutions, but I prayed a lot about it.

I can't include village pigs as a danger, but they were a nuisance as they were never penned up. One sow and her squealing babies tried to establish squatters' rights under our up-on-stilts house. They preferred the section of earth under our bedroom and after dark would noisily settle themselves. I didn't want the children to say they had been brought up with pigs sleeping under the bed! Our mattresses were on the floor and not too many feet away from the hogs, so I had a pig-poking stick capable of reaching through the cracks of the floor and routing them out. They would flee, protesting, into the night, only to return as soon as I settled down. As long as I was awake we would repeat the process!

There were snakes around, though not as many as you might expect for the village proper was kept clear of shrubs and grass. Sometimes we found centipedes and scorpions. One day for some unexplained reason I pulled down the mosquito nets, tied up over our beds during the day, while it was still light. I was so glad I did, for a scorpion was resting in the tucked-in part of the net. We did also have to keep our eyes open for such things as fuzzy caterpillars that left their irritating fuzz in your skin if you touched them. But we never had to worry about the children watching crime, violence, and the crudities of western civilization on TV, so things balanced out. And there were never any traffic problems in our isolated mountain homes.

Our children had the colds normal to childhood, were fractious when their molars came through, and suffered numerous fevers of unknown origin. During one rainy season when Larry was away and not even an oxcart could have plowed through the boggy trails, the girls were running such high temperatures that I had visions of having to hire people to carry them out to the motor road. I pored anxiously over the medical books trying to locate their symptoms. When they both blossomed out with measles, they had a delighted and relieved mother. In these circumstances I probably prayed more than I would have done at home, within telephone reach of a pediatric nurse. Yes, I worried sometimes, but my worries turned me to the Lord and reminded me that we needed continually to trust Him for the children's safety, growth and health. Today we have four grown-up children, all of average size, shape and well-being to prove they were not deprived in their youth.

My husband and I, on furlough in the States, were members of a panel at a missionary conference. A Bible school student stood up and asked: "When you send your children away to school, what Scripture can you give to justify this abandoning of your responsibilities as parents?" We were all too taken aback to give concrete answers. I don't remember what we finally said, but as missionary parents we had, of course, to think through this question.

It seemed to us that God had said we were to go into all the world to preach the Gospel, and His Word did not suggest that this command was limited to single people. Were we to assume that married people, called to this ministry, should remain childless in order to spare their children from the hazards of the mission field? My husband and I did not assume this. We believed that if it pleased God for us to go to Thailand, He would take responsibility not only for us but also for our children. I still believe that. "Lo, I am with you always, even to the end of the world," is not a promise for parents alone. It extends to the children. God promises to bless those who obey Him, and our children are included both in the obedience and the blessing.

In some places it is feasible for children to attend local schools. This was not possible for ours, who went to our mission boarding school, Chefoo, in the cool healthy mountains of Malaysia. They left at the age of five and a half, which was hard for them and for us. It would have been quite impossible apart from the assurance that it was the right thing to do — not the easy thing, but the right one. I myself had taught at Chefoo in China and had seen the school with adult eyes, and I knew it was a happy place.

A little girl going to Chefoo for the first time, seeing her mother's distress when they had to say goodbye, said cheerily: "Never mind, Mummy, I'll soon forget you!" There is a wry comfort in knowing that the children are soon thoroughly absorbed in their friends and in all the special delights planned for them. Our girls have said that once the parting was over they really loved school. Another small Chefooite said to her mother before they went to the airport: "Don't cry, Mummy. It doesn't help anything." I learned that it doesn't. When I longed for a glimpse of them or wondered if they were happy, and when the time between holidays seemed interminable, there was comfort in knowing that they were in the right place, the place that God had designed for them, and that God would not withhold from them anything that would benefit them.

Chefoo took them through six grades. Nowadays many of the Chefoo students go on to the Philippines to a Christian high school, but this was not an option in our day. When Marilyn finished at Chefoo we went on furlough, and upon our return to the field she aged eleven and Shirley at nine were left at home in one of our mission hostels in Canada. Before we left them I was frantic with worry. Were we doing the right thing for them? Would they be able to adjust to the new situation? Would they be unhappy? At that point the Lord brought to my mind the crossing of the Red Sea. Surely some mother hesitated on the bank, wondering fearfully if it was right to take their children into the path so recently parted for them. But as they went forward, knowing it was God who had made this strange way for them, they proved it was both safe and right.

God's normal pattern is for a child to be with his parents, but sometimes He fulfills His purpose in another way. If it is the Lord who opens a strange path, then it is right to walk in it, trusting His love and protection. Then it is right, not to abandon our parental duties as the Bible school student saw it, but rather, for a time, to delegate our parental authority to someone else.

This stand was tested, of course. Our children had their ups and downs like every normal teenager. Sometimes we knew about the "downs", and then it was harder to believe our decision was right. The Lord knew when I was wavering and unfailingly reminded me of applicable parts of His Word. If you were asked to name some Old Testament stalwarts, would your list include Moses, Samuel, Joseph and Daniel? They have something in common. Moses had only a few years in his godly home, and was then brought up in a pagan palace where God prepared him to deliver His people. The little boy that Hannah gave back to her Lord became God's faithful servant. He could have been influenced by Eli's godless sons, but the Lord guarded him. Joseph and Daniel were both dragged away from the family circle in their difficult teenage years, to live in the houses of the great and mighty, houses where God was not acknowledged. What Joseph's brothers planned as evil God planned for blessing to others, including the brothers themselves. Daniel witnessed to his faith before kings. I saw the faithfulness of God to these young people and I was encouraged to believe for mine.

A friend who prayed faithfully for our family wrote saying, "Sometimes M. (her teenage daughter) and I have great times together. She is on cloud nine and everything is right with her world. At other times she closes up and doesn't want advice or comfort or anything. Then I am shut up to my one resource — prayer to a loving Heavenly Father. And this resource is constantly open to you, whether you are in Canada, or separated from your children by the space of the Pacific Ocean." There was immense comfort, again and again, in turning over to Him the lives of the ones we cared about.

Do these last few paragraphs sound like the rationalization of a guilty conscience? They are not. They set forth the "Red Sea" through which we had to make our way. They are the convictions of one who believes God gives wisdom for our decisions, and above our decisions He is sovereign, working all things together for good.

I know many Christians at home feel as that Bible School student felt — that not only are we neglecting our duty to our children, but we are insensitive and unfeeling. For what kind of love is it that can so easily part with a child? But I know too that our own children do not accuse us of lack of love. Some day they may conceivably say we were mistaken in our interpretation of what obedience involved. But that we left them because we did not care about them — they will not accuse us of that. They know what it costs to be concerned about God's commands. Every furlough I went through the same thing, hoping wildly that something would happen so we could legitimately stay at home. Right to the final farewell I was still watching for God to intervene and spare us the separation. He did not do this, but He did pour in His grace, making our sorrow bearable.

When missionaries' children turn away from the Lord, people inevitably blame it on their separation from their parents. This could be a contributing factor, but it is not necessarily so. Can we assume that all children who stay with their parents will be found walking in God's paths? A look around the Christian community at home proves this is not a valid assumption. There are many other factors involved, not the least being that missionary kids, like other young people, have the power of choice.

I believe God wants missionary families on the mission field, especially in pioneer areas like North Thailand. After widowed Gill Orpin with her little son Murray had lived for a time in the Hmong village where Doe Jones was serving, Doe said that Gill's discipline of Murray and her loving care of him had been a real witness to the Christian families. Previously Doe had been teaching on the duties of Christian parents, but as she was single her words were not heeded. When Gill lived out the biblical teaching, parents *saw* what Doe had been talking about.

When I was a small girl I had the blessing of a large array of adoring uncles and aunts. Each summer we visited one another, and during the rest of the year letters and presents were reminders that I was loved. We all enjoyed the present that came each Christmas from a favorite uncle — huge dark brown boxes of chocolates, filled with maple walnuts, fruit creams and peppermint patties. When we came to Thailand with our five-month-old daughter we said goodbye to her own adoring circle of relatives, and felt a certain sense of deprivation that our children, except on furlough, would never enjoy the blessing I had as a child. How could relatives at a distance of thousands of miles add any love and security?

But I was wrong. I should have remembered the Lord's plain statement that when we forsake families for His sake He makes a hundred percent return. Our children have never lacked the loving care of mission "aunties and uncles." Once when living in a Lahu village Larry and I came down with dengue fever on the same afternoon, and it was Uncle Neville Long who took over the running of the household and the care of two small Peets. As the breadmaker was flat on her back, Uncle Neville made baking powder biscuits that resembled flat round bits of heavy cardboard, but Marilyn and Shirley said they were just like cookies and much tastier than Mother's baking! They liked the biscuits because they liked Uncle Neville.

One time Larry took Shirley and Gordon to Bangkok to deal with red tape, but on arrival he collapsed and had to be hustled into hospital. A telegram was sent to me but until I could get there the children were cared for by Auntie Elizabeth and Uncle Harry Gould. At that point I was in great awe of Uncle Harry, and I worried that our shy pair would be similarly ill at ease. When I arrived that same shy pair weren't particularly excited about seeing me. They informed me they loved being with the Goulds. Uncle Harry had been on night duty and had prowled around in the dark, finding Gordon's teddy bear for him whenever it fell out of bed. When we left for the furlough after which our two oldest would stay in Canada for the first time, Uncle Harry called the girls into his office and gave them each an envelope containing Canadian dollar bills, saying the money was to be spent when their parents returned to Thailand. Just before he died Uncle Harry wrote us a letter·in which he said, "I always loved your children." Yes, we were rich indeed.

Usually there were more aunties than uncles around. When our house was surrounded by a flood it was a vigilant auntie who retrieved a four-year-old non-swimming Peet who had fallen into the swirling waters. It seemed that there were always aunties on hand to admire and encourage and baby sit, to listen patiently to this fond mother talk about her children, to ooh and aah over photos received, chuckle over the unintentional humor in the kids' letters and be suitably impressed with the tales of their exploits. And some have taken our children into their prayer care. Our children have never lacked a host of loving relatives.

Chapter 10

Miss Taylor Built The Ark

MY MOTHER'S MAIDEN name was Taylor. Before her marriage she was great friends with a local minister's family, whose four-year-old John held her in esteem and affection. One day at family prayers, when John was not paying very much attention, questions were asked about the Bible story they had just read. "Who built the ark?" father asked. Knowing that there was no deed above the powers of his teacher friend John replied with assurance, "Miss Taylor built the ark."

We have many "Miss Taylors" in North Thailand. I don't want to sound like an advertisement for women's lib, but I can say with authority that I have nothing but the highest praise for the ministry of single ladies. I am confident that our "Miss Taylors" could, if called upon to do so, build a very respectable ark. Not that any of them have taken a course in ark building, though we have had a number of teachers, some nurses, a secretary and a draftsman. But their formal learning has not prepared them for such things as carrying pails of water one on each end of a pole, building fences, digging wells, repairing leaf roofs, supervising the construction of a house, dragging trees in from the forest, crossing rivers in full spate, carrying back packs heavy with full supplies up steep mountains, making cupboards and putting up shelves, killing snakes, and fending off dogs.

If I say the ladies have mastered these skills you may well picture a crowd of veritable Amazons. No. One has had back surgery, another multiple surgeries on a foot that still keeps her from complete freedom. Another — all of 4' 10" — strained her back carrying firewood and had to go home for treatment, but is now on the job again. One has arthritis and varicose veins. One is tall and willowy and looks fabulous in a long flowing gown sweeping down our Mission Home stairs. One is thin and delicate looking. None are strikingly athletic, and none are getting any younger. In fact one has recently become a pensioner in her native Wales. So the life they live has not been without personal cost.

I remember a Yao Christian leader visiting the Yao villages in which two of our single ladies regularly taught. It was the rainy season and the trails had achieved their utmost in horror. When he finally reached the end of his trip, exhausted, he said, "Ladies should not have to go on paths like this." Yao men are not chivalrous — their women are expected to do a full heavy day's work — but he could see that circuit demanded too much. A fellow missionary asked who then should do this necessary tribal teaching. There was no answer to that.

I have heard people say that because men have resisted God's call, women must do the work they should be doing. This suggests that it would be better if men were available, but since they are not we will have to take a substitute. I don't believe a word of it. God hasn't been defeated or been reduced to using "second best." I expect there are men at home who have resisted God's call, but that doesn't mean the women's ministry is a substitute for them. Ladies are on the mission field because God wants them there to do a job He has designed for them.

Some tribes do place cultural restrictions on a woman's ministry. For example, it is not a part of Shan culture for a woman to teach a man, though the older generation of Shan men would perhaps feel this more strongly than others. What helps them to accept women's teaching is the fact that missionaries aren't Shan anyway, so they don't need to be governed by the Shan laws. What would be a restriction for a Shan woman does not necessarily hinder a foreigner.

In the Yao religious world there is a teacher-student relationship involving more than teaching, and this close bond between two people would not be possible for a foreign woman and a tribal man. Someone asked a Yao church leader about a lady missionary unconnected with the Yao, whose Bible teaching gifts are evident to all. "What would be the Yao reaction to such a one teaching Yao men?" he asked. "A Yao man would not want to listen," was the firm reply. But that does not eliminate a woman's ministry. She has freedom to evangelize, to teach in an informal setting like sitting around the fire at night, to teach literacy, Bible geography, or singing — anything that would not involve this disciple-teacher relationship.

The White Hmong men have had more difficulty than the Blue Hmong in accepting women's ministry, but they do recognize that foreign women have had training that prepares them for sharing the Word. Once when the two Barbaras were hesitant about usurping authority, Blue Hmong Christian Noah encouraged them. "Don't hold back," he said, "You know things we don't know. No one will think it is wrong if you teach us."

Mrs. Doong Ye summed it up well. Two of the Hmong Christian men had broken with opium and then gone back to it, while their wives remained in fellowship with the Lord. When a missionary spoke about the possibility of them witnessing in other villages Mrs. Doong Ye replied, "The men have no face to go, so we will. It doesn't matter that we are only women because we are not speaking our own words, but the Lord's. The Lord's words are the same whether spoken by men or women." These were wise words. She wasn't trying to put herself above anyone else, for she knew her place in the Hmong scheme of things. Most tribal men regard women as inferior. A Canadian friend of mine was going out to fix a tractor. He didn't know what the trouble was, and as he went out the door his wife suggested a possible reason. "What does a woman know?" he called back, half in fun. After working all day he finally decided to try his wife's suggestion. She was right. Tribal men would agree with him: "What does a woman know?" But Mrs. Doong Ye had moved beyond man-made distinctions and she knew the power of the Word.

Our Miss Taylors often have to travel alone. The North Thailand field early decided that it was best to travel in twos, both for safety and also to fit in with Thai customs, for in Thailand a lady traveling by herself may not be up to any good. However, it is one thing to have a law and quite another to carry it out, and this one has been impossible to follow in practice. It is not realistic. Even if you have a fellow worker it is not at all certain that you can travel everywhere together.

Another ideal is that no one should live in a village without a fellow worker. But if we followed this ideal, some stations would have to be vacant, for there are not enough missionaries to go around. So some ladies are living alone in isolated villages, and this can be a lonely business. Fellowship with the local believers is a happy thing, of course, but it is not always possible to share deep personal needs, nor to speak of the problems of the work, especially if the believers are the problems! You long to pray with someone over these things, but no one is there. If your language is still at the beginning stages there are things you cannot explain, and some jokes simply can't be translated into another language.

Loneliness is not restricted to single people, of course. We all suffer from it at times. I can remember occasions when Larry was away from our Lahu village, and when I had only a child's vocabulary and was not really communicating. I would find myself watching the little path that led into the village, passionately longing for some foreign guest to appear, or to be able to escape. This does not sound spiritual, but it is human. Any wife will tell you that everything goes wrong when friend husband is away. The night the drunk man was vomiting on our porch and trying to get in, Larry was away. Another time we had left our Lahu home for a temporary lodging on the plain, at Consular orders. During that time our language teacher was killed, another man in the village wounded and our house plundered. When police came to tell us about it Larry was preaching in the Lahu hills, and the police insisted that I go with them to see what had been taken. A fellow missionary went with me, but it was an unpleasant trip. Things had a way of falling apart the minute Larry was out the door. I could almost count on the children being sick. The time the first Thailand Lahu believed, both our son Alan and I were really ill.

Living alone in a tribal village means that all the jobs that seem the easier for being shared must be done alone. There is no one to consult when the neighbor appears to be at death's door. Even if your fellow worker has no more medical sense than you, it helps to talk it over. Being alone means that you must take care of all the visitors. If there are two of you, one can talk with guests while the other gets on with cooking the noon rice. Alone, it has to wait until some impossible hour when you are free to get to it. If there are two of you, you might be able to put your feet up for fifteen minutes during the worst of the afternoon heat. Alone, you are always on call and this can be exhausting.

Margaret Clarkson in her book *So you're single*,[1] which is as helpful to married people as it is to singles, speaks of the way the Lord solves the problem of loneliness. "The companionship of Jesus Christ through the Holy Spirit is no myth. He is the first person I speak to in the morning and the last at night...

"We don't talk only of spiritual things, He and I, although that, of course, is part of each day's fellowship. We keep up a running conversation all day long, whatever I may be doing. I'm constantly needing His help with this problem, that undertaking, this attitude and that temptation, and it's always available. Together we share many a good book, concert, play or ballet, and many a good joke. Together we create a song, a poem, an evening dress or a pant suit, together plan an article or a book. My heart is constantly reaching up to Him in gratitude and praise by day and often far into the night. In return He gives Himself to me." Few missionaries in tribal houses will be

[1]Harold Shaw Publishers

designing evening dresses or pant suits — they are more likely to be wrestling with Lahu syntax or setting traps for rats — but the principle holds. He promises His continual presence.

I have been slow to learn what a practical thing this is, feeling that God was dealing with the vast concerns of the universe so how could I dare to intrude with my trivialities? But I am learning that I may read my letter aloud to Him, or talk things over with Him in the night hours when I cannot sleep. I even dare to tell Him how difficult I am finding my particular thorn in the flesh. I know He won't be bored or disinterested with the things that are important to me. He is incapable of getting tired of me. Amy Carmichael says, "We have far too poor a conception of the intimacy with our God which He desires should be habitual." It is this fellowship that makes possible the "aloneness" of missionary life.

Chapter 11

Sorrows Into Keys

THE THAILAND SUN was fiercely burning as my friend Ellen and her companion were trudging down a dusty Thai trail looking for opportunities to tell their good news. It was so hot that the local Thai women were trying to find some relief in the shade under their up-on-stilts houses. The two missionaries, themselves glad of a cooler spot, went to sit down beside them. After listening to their story for a while, one of the hearers remarked to Ellen, "I could be a Christian too if I had nothing to do but walk around and visit the neighbors!"

This was the usual attitude of the tribal people. Missionaries didn't clear land, or plant it, or weed rice fields; we didn't cut down trees or search in the jungle for pig food. We weren't dependent on rains for our rice. We did no work and had no problems. We just visited people. It was easy for *us* to be Christians. In the light of this attitude, our visible trials were a good thing. I am not an expert as I once thought I was in puzzling out God's purposes in what He brings into our lives. However, I am firmly convinced that God is almighty, wise and loving in all His dealings, and that He will use every circumstance for blessing.

Appendectomy, arthritis, bite from rabid cat, broken collar bone, broken wrist, bronchitis, chicken pox, dengue, dysentery, enteric fever, flu, measles, pneumonia, rheumatic fever, scarlet fever, open heart surgery, sciatica, TB, tonsillitis, typhus and worms. No, this is not a leaf from a medical journal which has strayed by mistake into these pages. It is a list of some of the illnesses our North Thailand missionary family has "enjoyed." We also suffered from headaches and colds and the many unidentified fevers which the tropics supply so abundantly. After one of our missionaries was bitten by a scorpion, the Lisu asked if she had cried with the pain as they do. They seemed to think that pain was not painful for us! So illness helped us to identify with them, showing that we are not superhuman beings but fellow sufferers who sometimes have to take to our beds, and who need God's comfort and grace for endurance.

New believers are often dismayed by the troubles that come to them. If our lives are cloudless the suffering tribesman cannot help thinking it is easy for a non-suffering missionary to talk about the grace of God. But when we have similar troubles we have the right to testify to God's grace and enabling. If from the center of our own personal storm we can say that God keeps our hearts at peace, then our testimony is valid.

Lew, a Hmong Christian, was held up on the trail and robbed of two valuable knives. The thieves gave him a beating and left him to limp his way home, where Leona Bair tried to comfort him. A few days later she too was beaten and threatened with a knife. Then Lew knew her words of comfort were not empty ones, but came from one who had herself experienced fear, pain and shock.

My copy of Amy Carmichael's book *Gold by Moonlight* is scruffy and worn, with many passages underlined. It has been a help through many years — in fact, when my husband sees me reading it he assumes I am in some kind of distress! Amy Carmichael's life was full of trials in which she proved that God was completely trustworthy. She writes, "The attempt of the evil one to destroy you will react upon himself, perhaps by weakening his grip on another soul, perhaps by furnishing you with the key to the confidence of one who needs your help — for all the deeper experiences of sorrow and comfort, temptation and victory, sooner or later turn to keys." We have often proved the truth of this.

When Vang Vu's body was found on a mountain trail, it was Gillian Orpin who was able to tell his wife that God takes loving care of widows. Gill had the right to say this, for her husband had been killed on a similar mountain path in that same area. She had paid the necessary price to become a comforter of others.

The Wyss family had only just settled into an Akha village when to their disappointment a number of Akha families, including the ones who had been showing an interest in the Gospel, suddenly moved away. Almost immediately some very undesirable outsiders moved in to the partially-vacated village. From then on the nights were filled with noisy gambling. All the men had guns and when they were drunk they were even more careless than usual in handling their firearms. No one felt safe, and the women did not dare to be outside after dusk. It was not merely unpleasant but dangerous. Peter and Ruth Wyss prayed earnestly, and it was not long before the Border Police visited the village, confiscated the dice, destroyed the gambling tables and ordered the prostitutes to leave. When the last intruder had gone everyone breathed a sigh of relief. Out of this distress came positive good, for the Wysses found these shared difficulties had united them with the Akha people. There was now a closeness that no amount of comfortable living could have brought about.

Heinz and Christiane Mayer had an even nastier experience. It had started as an ordinary week, with the usual group meeting on Sunday for worship and teaching when Heinz had spoken about God's deliverance of Moses. Monday evening Christiane was feeding baby Sarah, supper was on the table, and two-year-old David was waiting for his daddy to join them in eating. Heinz himself was out on the porch, treating a Karen lad with a deeply embedded splinter in his foot. Just as he finished, two strangers came up on the porch, one of whom said he had a fever. Heinz took his pulse and found it normal, but decided to give him malaria medicine as nearly everybody has malaria. When he came out with glasses of water and the pills, a third stranger had arrived and was carefully examining a gospel poster on the porch. The young man took the pills Heinz offered him but hesitated about swallowing them, and then suddenly grabbed Heinz while three more men, fully armed, rushed up the porch step. One stuck a gun in Heinz's ribs, warning him to be quiet and to tell them where the money and guns were stored.

Heinz called out to Christiane in a low voice, and though she didn't hear what he said his tone warned her something was wrong, so she had a moment to prepare before the men came into the kitchen. One of them said in faltering English, "We want money. Sorry, sorry, we want money." Little David, seeing one of them holding a knife at his mother's back, began to cry, and his fears were not allayed when another knife-wielding fellow picked him up. By this time Heinz had his hands tied behind his back and was tethered to a pillar on the porch with yet another pistol pressed against his forehead.

The Karen lad with the foot injury had slipped off into the dusk and run for help, and now the men of the village, also with their guns, came rushing to defend their missionaries. At the robbers' command, Heinz called out urgently to them, "Don't shoot or I will be killed!" The robbers found some money, a watch and the tape recorder in the house, and one man collected the spoils while another, holding David high in the air so the Karen could see what he was doing, hurried down the steps. Meanwhile yet another was tramping back and forth, wildly waving his gun. Christiane, still holding the baby, was forced down the steps too. Finally Heinz was untied and the robbers used the family as a human buffer, jerking them back and forth to protect themselves from the bullets which had begun to fly, as they made their way into the jungle.

They were forced to run through the jungle, up a hill and through a creek, until Christiane could go no further. When she fell they left her and ran on. Heinz somehow managed to get hold of David, who was crying with terror, and when Heinz fell they left him too and fled into the darkness. He crawled over to where Christiane and the baby were lying.

At last the Karen found the still dazed family, and escorted them back to the house. They still could not believe they were safe. Everybody crowded round, murmuring sympathetically, the women stroking Christiane and the children and trying to comfort them. David, his tears now dried, wanted to sing the Swiss equivalent of *Ring around a rosy*, and then the elders prayed and thanked God for His deliverance. Everyone realized that the God who had been with Moses had now also been with them. People stayed till midnight, talking, singing and reading the Word. Even when, exhausted, they finally went to their own homes, they left five armed men to guard the house.

Heinz and Christiane, uncertain that the affair was really ended, made ready for another session in the forest before locking themselves in. They lay down fully dressed and turned to the Lord's Word, taking turns in reading chapters aloud. The Lord drew near to them as they read Ezekiel 34:25,28,30, which in their Swiss German version said: "I want to make a covenant of peace with them, and chase the evil animals out of the country, so that they may be able to sleep in the forest. I want to make them a blessing and the surrounding hills a blessing. And they shall not be a prey to the heathen any more nor shall the wild animals of the land eat them. This way they shall know that I, the Lord God, am with them, and that they, the house of Israel, are my people, saith the Lord. You are the sheep of my flock; I am your God saith God the Lord."

They had known fear, for they had expected to be killed. But they had also known that God was in control. He had spared their lives so the material loss seemed small, and many reasons for praise came into their minds as they relived the traumatic evening. Heinz marveled that he had known how to say in Karen, "Don't shoot or I will be killed." That sentence certainly wasn't in their language lessons so far! They had experienced the love and concern of the villagers, and their willingness to defend them. The Karen are not usually demonstrative but one woman had put her arm around Christiane in loving thanks that they were not hurt.

Next morning one of the robbers was found lying unconscious near the stream. He had been shot. The Karen found it hard to understand that the Mayers forbade any vengeance being taken, and that they hurried to give first aid. It was Heinz's opportunity to speak of the Christian duty to love your enemies. Unfortunately the robber was beyond help and soon died.

The Christian villagers assumed the Mayers would want to move to a safer area, and asked them anxiously, "Do you still love us? Will you stay?" When Heinz and Christiane assured them, "Yes, we still love you. We have no intention of leaving," a new bond of love drew them all together. The terrible episode had welded their relationship and made them as one, a great gain that the enemy of souls did not intend.

Heinz and Christiane felt the effects of the shock for some time. After their year's furlough at home I asked how it was for them to return. Christiane told me God had given them peace, but sometimes fear did recur. The unexpected arrival of strangers or the sound of shooting made their hearts thump a bit; but they are willing for this in order to give God's Word to these people who are now "their people."

Doe Jones and Doris Whitelock had locked up their house in their Hmong village and journeyed down to Chiang Mai. When they reached home again after a long tiring climb in the heat, they found the house had been broken into. Most of their things were gone — not just radio and record player but many things of small value that are irreplaceable on the mountain.

Doe wrote about that experience: "How big the little things seem at such a time. Things like the clothes we left for washing on our return and which the thieves missed, so we had a change of clothes. Only one hot water bottle taken and one left, one blanket left and the loan of one by a Christian. And there are big things which are very precious to us, the Lord's gracious giving of wonderful peace and joy; we haven't had to force ourselves to be cheerful; on Sunday there was a closeness with the Christians which drew us all together in worship and there is the confident assurance that while men have done this to us for evil yet the Lord means it for good." Doris and Doe had taught that God can be trusted through difficult days. The Hmong believers now saw the teaching *applied* in these two missionary lives, and this object lesson was worth any number of words.

These two ladies had other opportunities to "take joyfully the spoiling of their goods," including the night their house was set on fire. Doe wakened and smelled smoke, but sleepily thought, "Doris can't sleep and she's stirring up the fire to make a cup of tea." But the noise of the crackling flames grew louder and she realized that it involved more than a cup of tea! She roused Doris and the two of them tried to put out the flames, but it was beyond them, and when they called to the neighbors for help no one responded. At last they ran to the home of one of the

Christians, who soon had it under control. Later they learned that some Communists had ordered the Hmong to set fire to the house, in the hope that the missionaries would die in the fire. This explained the lack of response from the neighbors, who knew what had been done and were afraid to get involved. It is bad enough to be the victim of a fire that starts from natural causes, but it is much more traumatic to know the fire was deliberately set to injure and kill. Everyone knew that the attempt might be repeated, and for Doe and Doris the crackle of a fire brought back the alarms of that night. But they didn't leave the village, and again the Christians saw that God is able to carry His children through every difficulty He asks them to experience, giving them patient endurance.

One Sunday, when the two Barbaras were meeting with Hmong Christians in a village near to their home, their house and all its contents were burned to the ground. Even the green papayas on the trees near the blaze ripened! In the charred remains of the house they found a watermelon that had shot out of the fridge when it exploded, now cooked to a kind of marmalade. Everything else was in ashes. Whether the fire started naturally or was "helped" could not be proven, and in any case proof would not bring back all that was destroyed. This included stacks of lessons for the theological education by extension program, result of hundreds of hours of hard work. God gave them the grace to start these all over again, and eventually the girls testified that the new materials were an improvement over the original ones. But that comfort only came much later. At the time, the Lord helped His two servants to demonstrate that through any loss He is our gain; our life does not consist of the abundance of things we possess. We who know Him have an imperishable treasure.

God never wastes our time. His dealings with us are purposeful. He continually demonstrates the proof of His Word which says that *all* things (without any exception) work together for good. Samuel Rutherford, wise in the ways of his God, said, "He is no idle husbandman. He purposeth a crop."

Chapter 12

The Picayune

FIRES, MURDER, ROBBERY — these trials are of crisis proportions. But what of the small pinpricks, troubles so small you are ashamed to call them troubles? The picayune was originally a coin of small value used in the southern United States, and the word has come to denote anything trivial or petty or small-minded. If you keep adding to your collection of the picayune, you could amass a large sum of "small coins." It may take more grace to live contentedly with a daily collection of small ills than to face a thief or a blazing house.

One small and continued trial for me was the number of hours devoted to the mechanics of living. I had had a vague picture of missionary life as one long sermon which I would preach to attentive listeners. I hadn't considered eating and drinking and laundry as being part of a missionary career. Nowadays filters to purify drinking water are available, but we had to boil the gallons of water needed in the tropics. It sounds petty to fuss over a job that even the most uninspired house-wife can do, but a surprising amount of time was needed to get the water boiled, then cool enough to drink.

Tribal village life seemed to fill up with hours of the mundane. All the laundry, for example, and there was such a pile of it every day in that heat, had to be done by hand in the stream. Our kids thought washing clothes in the stream was a lark, but I just found it inconvenient — I didn't want to get wet, and there was no place to put your soap or your clean laundry, and it was a back-breaking chore. Sometimes I had a Lahu girl that we paid to help, but even so the day seemed to be crowded with unimportant things.

I found this terribly frustrating, for I assumed that housework wasn't "spiritual" work. I would come to the end of my day feeling that the only proper work I had done was to teach a literacy class and have my language lesson. Teaching Lahu children to read and mastering the language was "sacred", but feeding my family and keeping them clean and happy was "secular." I finally realized this was nonsense. Both were necessary parts of my day, equally under the blessing of God.

I had not reckoned either on the fact that closeness to the people would mean such a lack of privacy. We began by living in Thai style houses, which are built to let in as much air and light as possible. Your neighbor's conversation comes into your house with the light and air. You must share the smell of their cooking, and you choke and splutter as the peppers and garlic fry! Since you can't bear to close a window or a door because of the heat, you may have the privilege of listening to your neighbor's radio played all day long at ear-deafening levels. You can enjoy their parties and, if they are the cantankerous variety, their quarrels. This works two ways, of course — if you quarrel, they can hear you!

In the tribal village we had company all day long. The minute we opened the door early in the morning the children would come in. They were not noisy, they were just there, observing everything that went on. In the evenings and on Sundays when the Lahu, being Christians, were in the village and not in their fields, the adults came. We wanted this, of course, for the evening is prime time for missionary work. After the first Akha families believed, Peter and Jean Nightingale had a meeting in their house every single night, for literacy, teaching and fellowship. Rain or shine, tired or not, whether other work was pressing or not, Peter and Jean gave their evening hours to the Akha believers, and the Christians flourished. This kind of people-contact was of eternal profit. The problem was the idlers who sat on the floor and stared. Everyone who had nothing to do did it at our house!

It is contrary to tribal custom to stay in a neighbor's house at meals but tribal law is suspended for foreigners, for the impulse to watch us eat is well-nigh irresistible. I almost hated meals. I am not sure why this is so irritating, but most lady missionaries share my antipathy to being observed as we take nourishment. I often had a little circle of "admirers" watching also as I did the dishes or prepared the food. The amount of frustration I felt was regulated by my state of grace. "Why didn't you take the opportunity to preach?" you may ask. The main reason was that my language was not sufficient for extemporaneous sermons. I was still carefully memorizing statements about the Gospel. But also, I cannot be depended on to have edifying thoughts when I am washing greasy plates in a teaspoon of water, or picking weevils out of the rice.

Is it sinful to feel the loss of your privacy? I often wrestled with this. The resentment that at times welled up through a day of feeling like a monkey in a cage was wrong — that was clear. I know some sociable westerners who enjoy having people around all day, but we are not all made that way. I was interested to read Marcia Davenport's book *Too Strong For Fantasy*,[1] in which she contends that some people are born really unable to share close living quarters. "The inability to adjust...is not necessarily selfishness or stubborness, though it may be...There is a temperament which requires at times to be alone." This "physically solitary nature", as she calls it, is bound to suffer in a tribal village. Those of us who, perhaps unduly, value our privacy, especially need prayer that we will respond biblically to the situation. Constantly interacting with people is emotionally exhausting, but missionaries can happily accept that when people are being helped. It is harder to feel happy that you and your home are just "entertainment value", on exhibition to relieve local boredom.

---

[1]Charles Scribners

Many years of my life have been spent hostessing in our various Mission Homes, and during those years the Lord gave me many opportunities to learn the lesson that there need be no division between sacred and secular. There was a day when I had tramped around the Chiang Mai market buying pork and chicken for the Mission Home and for guests who would be taking supplies of food up to the holiday cottage on the mountain. The marketing loads were always heavy, and always it seemed a long walk to the place where I could catch a small *song tao* to deposit me and my bundles at the Mission Home gate. When I read my Bible that evening, my eyes fell on the words, "Labor not for the meat that perisheth." It was the last straw. I shed self-pitying tears, and it was a few hours before my sense of humor revived and I could laugh at my own misinterpretation of the meaning of Scripture. God was not rebuking me for buying meat for His servants; even forays in the market were part of His work for me.

More often when I was struggling over the amount of time spent on the "dailyness" of life, His Word did meet my particular need. At one point I had been using every available moment to plan a wedding for two of our young missionaries. The reception and meal were my responsibilities and all the out-of-town guests would be staying with us, so there was much to plan. One evening as I was wondering if I was spending too much time on this my regular reading included the reassuring words: "As we have opportunity let us do good to all men, and especially to those who are of the household of faith." Yes, it was right to plan carefully so that for the bride and groom it would be the best of possible days. It turned out to be just that, with only one small hitch. Someone cut her thumb and bled into the punch before we could help her. As there was no other punch available, and it was pink anyway, we decided to offer our sanguinary drink and say nothing about it. Everyone enjoyed it and suffered no ill effects!

I function well with a carefully planned schedule, and Mission Home days were made up of interruptions and unplanned duties, so I was not always at my psychological best. The erratic arrival and departure of guests was one of my "picayunes." Communication from a tribal village is difficult and often folk could not let us know when they were coming — I had no trouble with that. It was the folk who either forgot or neglected to advise us that troubled me. And even the most faithful communicators of their travel plans often didn't say how long they would stay. I would not know if they wanted just a noon meal, or room and board for two weeks, and I could not bring myself to say to guests when they arrived on our doorstep: "When are you leaving?"

And then there were the folk who said they would be in for lunch and didn't turn up, and others who said they wouldn't be in for lunch and who did turn up. More than once we prepared a huge meal for Lahu guests who left for home before they ate it, leaving us with all that food, liberally peppered to suit Lahu palates. I often fussed over the prospect of more guests than mattresses, and yet I found many times that the Lord arranged things so that a tidy room with welcoming orchids was available for each tired guest. God had a schedule even if I couldn't stick to mine, and I began to learn the folly of fussing over *my* plans. God's thought for me is to live by faith in Him; my security is in Him, not in checking off completed duties on my housework list. God never intended life to be full of fuss over the picayune.

We all have our areas of sensitivity and fellow workers may not realize the things that easily wound us. When I was hostess at the Mission Home, each missionary had part of a cupboard for storing things so that town clothes may stay in town and not have to be lugged out to the villages. But most guests started on their homeward journey early in the morning and so the laundry for that day had to be put away by the hostess. That is all a simple enough procedure. However, an OMF hostess "law" was that your laundry must be marked with your own name, so that it was easy to identify and put in its proper place. Quite a few of my dear fellow missionaries did not heed my "law", and on days when seven or eight people left I was faced with masses of clothes to put away somewhere. The ladies' dresses I could usually identify, but the men's slacks and people's under-clothes were more difficult.

Getting more and more irritated, I fastened a laundry marker on a string with a polite sign asking people to mark their clothes. It did not a bit of good, and I went around muttering about OMFers who can't even read. The sight of the unused laundry marker began to enrage me. Putting away the laundry, coming as it did at the end of hot busy days, became a hated chore. As I mused on the reasons for people not obliging in this simple matter, it seemed like a slight. After all, I was merely a hostess. I was already sensitive about my work, feeling it wasn't very spiritual in contrast to the pioneer efforts of the people whose clothes I was struggling with. My self-pity said that no one cared about the use of my time; no one minded if the job took three times as long as was necessary. A simple solution would have been to announce publicly that unmarked laundry was defeating me, but I am a Mrs. Milque-toast and avoid confrontation, so I chose to fume. Sometimes I would be aware of my ungracious attitude and I would ask the Lord to help me put the clothes away *gladly*. He did give help when I asked, but I didn't really want help as much as I wanted those clothes marked. One day, seething inwardly, I took some clothes whose owner I knew and marked them myself with her name, and not very tidily either. It speaks well for the owner's sanctification, for to this day she magnanimously regards me as a friend.

Why do I tell such a pathetically unimportant story? Because I believe that some of the biggest battles in relationships are fought on just such unimportant grounds. I have heard a heated discussion on how long to boil a soft-boiled egg. In mission work in Canada I remember arguing fiercely with my fellow worker as to the way of spiritual victory. We were upset with each other for a time until finally the Lord, or our sense of humor, took over and we realized that if either of us knew the way of victory we certainly were not walking in it!

Some of the issues of disagreement have been more important than eggs. What script should be used in tribal languages? This was a very "hot potato" in the early days, and people functioned almost as antagonists. Very few of us are able to discuss differences of opinion without emotional overtones, without feeling threatened. We inherited Lahu Scriptures already in an English script so we were spared the script fight, but the other battles swirled round our heads. The art of disagreeing without being disagreeable has to be learned, and not all of us have finished our lessons in this department. I myself am not bright enough to be a controversialist, so it was natural timidity and not spiritual attainment that kept me mostly quiet during those discussions on work methods; I sat through them hating every minute of it.

People at home may assume that missionaries automatically live in peace and harmony; but nothing could be farther from the truth! Harmony is never achieved easily or automatically. I think of two ladies who worked together. One was a choleric — quick to make decisions, quick to attack a problem and see the solution. The other was phlegmatic and found decisions painful. She had the power to see all the obstacles, as well as some imagined ones, in the road, and liked to examine all the possibilities thoroughly, weighing the options with maddening deliberation. The first one wanted to do the medical work at a set time and then put the medical supplies away for the day. The other didn't object to having patients amble in any time, and was prepared to sit and pass the time of day with anyone who wanted to talk. One wanted all projects perfect in every detail, the other felt there were so many urgent jobs to be done that some perfection would have to be sacrificed. How could these two, with opposite approaches to every aspect of life, work in harmony? They could not, apart from the Lord. Their unity lay in subjection to Him and He brought them through. But there were stresses and strains.

I love the North Thailand gang dearly and to be part of the family for nearly thirty years has brought me much joy. I am not suggesting that we are a particularly quarrelsome, vituperative group. It is just that we are people, constantly needing a renewal of love for our Lord and His children. One of my Snoopy posters says: "I love all mankind. It is people I can't stand." Even Snoopy knows that love is not a vague diffused feeling for the world in general, but something lived out in close relationships with people who don't mark their laundry. Mr. Hoste, director of our Mission in China days, used to pray with his wife that they would love one another. This offended her and she protested finally, "Why do you pray that, as though we didn't love each other?" "Because", he said, "Satan always attacks that which is of God."

We do love each other in North Thailand but Satan constantly attacks, making small pinpricks of annoyance grow and fester until they are like tropical sores, difficult to heal. It is easy to have a critical heart, and then to share the criticism with someone else. This helps Satan do his work of accusing the brethren, and does incalculable harm. And the disloyalty effectively quenches fellowship. We specially appreciated a fellow missionary who came and spoke plainly but graciously, questioning decisions my husband, as superintendent, had made. Because of this it was possible to explain the reasons, and though disagreement might continue there was no break in fellowship. We need enlarged capacities for love — a continued appreciation of one another, a quiet acceptance of the foibles and failings of our fellow workers, the power to happily put away unmarked laundry because we love the owners of the clothes.

All of us know people who have irritating ways. They may be Christians and well meaning, and still have the knack of bringing out the worst in us. What would you do if you had to work closely with them, not just from 9 to 5 Monday through Friday, but every day and all day? If you had to see them first thing in the morning and last thing at night, with no escape ever? Unless you have experienced it you can hardly realize the closeness of relationship necessary in a tribal situation. There is no concert hall or library in the village. You are miles from other missionaries. The two of you must eat three meals together every day. The houses are small and your only escape is a bit of bedroom, but privacy is minimal in a bamboo house so you can rarely be alone.

Married couples can find that isolation puts strains on their marriage. What about single folk who must live together? Their partners are chosen for them and there is little possibility of change. In the Thai-speaking areas it is easier to arrange change, but each tribal team is very small in number. A Lahu speaker is no use in a Yao village, and if you have learned Akha you can't move to a Hmong village. Your language fixes you almost irrevocably. You are stuck. Both married couples and single folk must tackle this problem of relationships in a confined area. We are told that some marriages founder over how the toothpaste tube is handled. In the narrow setting of tribal life trifles can seem titanic, the picayune really painful.

Why is it that we so often fail to walk victoriously through our small trials? Is it because we imagine we ought to be adequate for the daily cares of life and so try to manage under our own steam? We quickly call on the Lord in time of crisis for then we know we can't cope, but we hardly like to bother the Lord with trifles. And our trifles accumulate until we are overwhelmed and frantic. We all know it's not sensible to make a mountain out of a molehill, but if we collect enough molehills we could build a mountain. But God's Word tells us that in knowing Him we have everything pertaining to life and godliness. Provision has already been made for us to cope with the picayune.

Jesus said that one of the distinguishing marks of His disciples was love, and we want our tribal folk to know His love. What if in missionary lives they can't see the distinguishing mark? They don't notice our learning or the sacrifices we have made to go to their village. They don't know we have made any, for who wouldn't want to live in their mountains? But they can recognize love and be drawn to its source. If a saint is a person who makes it easier for others to believe in God, then missionaries need help. They cannot make it on their own.

"First we must believe that Christ loves us just as we are. We are impatient, grumpy, because we really hate ourselves. It is difficult to believe that right now, in the light of what we have just done, God loves us as much as He says He does. When I find myself critical of people I live with at home or at work, I don't need more patience but rather time alone to let God remind me of His love for me. When I know I am loved by Him and am forgiven for present failures, then I find the things that have been so irritating in my family members become trivial."[2]

This matter of loving relationships involves knowing God's love for me. There was a time when I did not understand this. Yes, I worked at loving people because the Word urged its importance. But things began to change the day I realized that God's love was unconditional. It did not depend on my fine spiritual performance, or fade when my performance was less than fine or spiritual. God's unconditional love for me — yes, for me, foolish and weak as I am — transformed my attitude toward myself. I was of value to God, one of His dearly loved children. This began to free me from the chains of self-hate and self-criticism, and His love is releasing me to respond to Him and to love others in a new way. God may provide many "inconvenient opportunities to love" when we work together on the mission field, but the enjoyment of His love enables us to make use of those opportunities. Arthur Way translates Romans 5:5 "the brimming river of God's love has already overflowed into our hearts, on-drawn by the Holy Spirit, which He has given us." If we are delighting in the brimming river the "problems" will cease to be problems.

---

[2]From *Living the Adventure* by Keith Miller and Bruce Larsen (Word Books)

Amy Carmichael's prayer sums it all up:
"For love, brave love that ventureth,
For love that faileth not, I come,
For love that never wearieth,
Nor findeth burdens burdensome.
O Love that light'nest all my ways
Within, without, below, above,
Flow through the minutes of my days,
The sum of all my life be love."[3]

---

[3]Wings

Chapter 13

Our Ancient Foe

THAILAND IS DOTTED with 20,000 beautiful temples, their inlaid glass of many shades and their gold and red paint glistening in the sun. Especially in the small villages life revolves around the temple. The festivals, which are as colourful as the temples, have religious significance but are also a lot of fun. As in every religion there are the devout, who follow the Buddhist precepts as closely as they can, scrupulously observe the holy days, avoid taking life (even of mosquitoes), give generously to the temples and help feed the priests. If you get up early enough, you will see single-file processions of saffron-robed priests walking barefoot along the streets, each carrying his bowl into which people along the road place their offerings of rice and other food. The food is, of course, of the best quality, but I have often wondered what that conglomeration of rice tastes like. However, whether ardently religious or not, all are concerned to make merit, or at least to avoid demerit, for the amount of *boon* or "merit" accumulated here and now affects your state in the next stage of reincarnation. A friend told us once that he had never been sick in his life so he must have acquired a lot of merit. Going into the priesthood, even for a short time, is a meritorious act. Even royalty conforms, and both the present King and his son have spent their fifteen days in the priesthood.

Any uninstructed tourist might feel that the Thai are very careful to look after their pet birds. But what appears to be an ornate bird house in the yard of most homes and even in front of government buildings is, in reality, a carefully tended spirit house, where flowers, rice, and sweets are offered. We had a spirit house in our yard once — the landlord refused to have it removed for he felt this would endanger him and his family, so there it stayed in a state of neglect and disrepair. When our small children were sick our language teacher rebuked us, saying it was because we had offended the spirits by refusing to make offerings.

Although the tribal people do not have spirit houses, they would have shared our teacher's diagnosis that we had given offense to the spirits. For them all of life, from birth to death and every intervening stage, is governed and influenced by spiritual powers. This is a bitter bondage. People who talk blithely about the "happy animist" who should be left to his own spiritual ways cannot have understood the burden that animism imposed.

Some Hmong are planning to start on a journey. If something accidentally falls off a shelf or a table, the trip must be postponed to a time more pleasing to the spirits. Or if the journey has started and a deer crosses the path, or a tree falls across it, the Hmong must return home at this sign of the spirits' displeasure. If a certain bird calls they must go back immediately even if they are near their destination.

If someone sneezes on the trail, the Karen know they must be cautious, and if the sneeze is repeated they must go back to the place they started from. Heinz Mayer is an early morning sneezer, and this has, at times, been highly embarrassing! However, the Christian Karen are beginning to see that these signs need have no power over them. Heinz had hired some local Karen men to walk out to their nearest market town to meet a Karen teacher and escort him back. But the morning they were to leave, something happened, a taboo so frightening they would not tell Heinz what it was. Even the Christians were fearful. Finally Heinz said he would go himself, and suggested that the headman's fourteen-year-old son should be his companion. A reluctant consent was given. What terrors filled the heart of that teenager? But the two walked to the market one day, met the teacher and returned with him safely the following day.

This was a very helpful object lesson for the Christians. Learning of their freedom in Christ is a progressive thing. If all your forebears have been filled with fear over these omens, all your relatives and neighbors know the terror of offending the spirits, and you yourself have been given this heritage of fear, it may take time for the power of that fear to be dispelled.

A Karen dies. The family know the spirits are unhappy, so the house must be abandoned and a new one built. The Karen also believe that when they are frightened part of their spirit disappears. If they are alarmed in the forest they must later return to the same spot and place a few chicken feathers there as a symbol of sacrifice. The Mayers' dog barked at some Karen and frightened them — later blood was sprinkled near the fence to appease the demon involved.

Most of the tribal groups have a demon priest or *shaman* who is responsible for all the religious affairs of the village. He is the mouthpiece of the spirits, advising about the ceremonies to be performed for averting their anger. He reads omens, interpreting their meaning so that the people concerned can be obedient. His predictions about calamity often do come to pass. And he has the power to accuse and curse wrongdoers, which is sometimes possessed by laymen too.

A young Hmong couple believed in the Lord. The husband's older brother, who is a demon priest, has always hated Christians, and when his brother believed he was furious. He told the couple: "Within three days, your baby will die." As far as one could see, the baby was perfectly well, but soon he took sick. The parents panicked. They had had no experience of the Lord's protection, and all their instincts said: "We have offended the spirits. Our baby is cursed and we must quickly repair the damage." They turned away from the Lord and did demon worship, but the baby died within the three days. People intent on proving that it is the fear of the curse that kills have nothing to say here, for the baby knew nothing of the matter. If only the parents could have allowed the Lord to show His power to protect them! But today they still live in their bondage, unaware that God does have freedom for them.

It is the demon priest who determines when a house or a whole village is under taboo so that no one may leave or enter it. On one occasion we had made a lengthy boat trip and sloshed our way through streams and rice fields, and were feeling relieved that the Lahu village where we were to spend the weekend was within hailing distance. And then we saw in the path a square of plaited bamboo tied to a short bamboo pole. It was a taboo sign.

We knew that some outsiders who had paid no attention to a similar taboo, entering the village and staying the night there, had been quietly disposed of on the trail next morning. So it was a serious matter, but it was too late to go home and we did not relish a night in the forest. A teenager guarding the place disappeared to report our arrival to the demon priest, who sent word that we could stay the night at Eh Shai's house. Eh Shai and his wife, who were Christians, lived in the first house along the path into the village proper. We were not to go any further into the village nor go to any other house, and we were to leave first thing in the morning. We did what we were told. We had fellowship with Eh Shai's family, but in a sense it seemed like a wasted visit, especially since a friend had come with us to "see" the Lahu work! We reminded ourselves though, that the Lord doesn't waste our time. And in that visit, we saw again the power that binds the Lahu.

Not all broken taboos are treated with such severity, and sometimes the tribal folk themselves found ways of circumventing them. Once when Doe Jones had been asked to help a sick child in a house that was taboo, she was told to come after dark when the spirits wouldn't see her. And on other occasions a board or two would be pulled off the side of the house so she could squeeze in that way. If she wasn't seen going through the conventional entrance, the sin might be overlooked.

The life of an Akha is hedged with prohibitions. Their village must be some distance from a stream, for to have one running through the village would offend the spirits. This is a great inconvenience, as the stream is their sole water source. It is also forbidden to plant papaya or banana trees within the demon gates that guard the entrance to non-Christian villages. It has been an eye opener to the onlookers when Christian villages are built along a stream and papayas and bananas flourish in people's gardens.

These laws are a nuisance but harmless; there are others that are more disturbing. The Akha believe that the birth of twins or of a deformed baby is an indication of the spirits' extreme displeasure. They are regarded as "human rejects", and the father must press a mixture of rice husks and ashes into the baby's nose and mouth until he suffocates. The Akha are a gentle people and their babies are precious to them, but this terrible necessity is laid upon them.

A few years ago, a Sgaw Karen headman had taken part in the three-times-a-year demon ceremony required of all adult males. A chicken was killed and the bones revealed a bad omen. He should have made another sacrifice but he didn't, and he broke another taboo also by eating the chicken that had given a bad omen. He died the next day. Heart attack? Coincidence? This death after a failure to comply with the demons' wish is not an isolated case.

The demon priest then consulted the spirits and found they were so offended at this disregard of their laws that any succeeding headman in that village would die. To avoid this the village moved to a new area, splitting up into three locations with a new headman for each. One of these men, Pha Ra Hae, was most concerned to do all that the demons required. Didn't his own safety and that of his village demand it? He was punctilious about the spirit ceremonies, and had more and more contact with the spirits until he felt they were controlling him. One day the spirits ordered him to take a knife, cut his throat and die. He told his family, and they did not dare to argue or try to prevent him. If the spirits had spoken, then obedience was the only possible course. Fully expecting to die, he slashed his own throat. The gaping wound bled copiously, but he did not die, to his own amazement and that of the people who had watched him do it.

Soon after this a family in his village believed in the Lord, and Pha Ra Hae became interested in the things they were talking about. One evening when the missionaries were visiting he invited Heinz Mayer to come and teach him. Heinz pointed out that God had spared his natural life so that he might receive spiritual life. To the neighbors that had gathered, Pha Ra Hae told the whole story, almost as though he were thinking it through for himself. In the telling, he became convinced that God is mightier than the demons. So that very evening all the things used in spirit worship — the pots and bamboo spoons and the pipe for calling the demon — were gathered into a heap and burned, while the Christians sang hymns about God's power to protect. They needed this assurance, for it is a frightening step to take. Pha Ra Hae and his wife and seven children turned away from the old burdensome life to be free in the Lord.

Since that time all the family, except for the oldest son, have held firmly to the faith. They have had trials. First a young son-in-law died, and then five of his nine buffalo. But Pha Ra Hae has not turned back even though he is illiterate and cannot read God's Word for himself. He still has an open hole in his windpipe and asthma complicates his breathing, but he belongs to the Lord who has taken him out of the kingdom of darkness.

What should a missionary teach a new believer about taboos and omens? God's Word assures us that in the Lord we have a refuge from Satan's attack, and that God's children are freed from bondage. A tribal Christian can pound his rice or look for firewood on a taboo day. He is free to point at the moon and not fear death, as would a non-Christian Hmong. What a relief when the tribal believer knows he is truly free, and that the old fears needn't haunt him. Yes, he has liberty — but he lives beside heathen who are not free and who fear they may be included in the demons' displeasure at the breaking of taboos. If a Christian were to venture into a home under taboo, the members of that family would be very angry, and any accident thereafter would be blamed on him. The apostle Paul said, in effect, that there might be times when, for conscience sake, a taboo must be broken. But he was also aware of the fears and sensibilities of others, and for their sakes he avoided giving offense.

Much of this could be dismissed as superstition and groundless fear. If it is just a matter of superstition then a short educational course for tribal people should put everything straight. There *is* superstition, certainly. But can death after disregard of omens be coincidence? After a while, when the "coincidences" accumulate, you are forced to take a second look, and to realize that behind the omens, taboos and curses stands an enemy. "We are up against the unseen power that controls this dark world, and spiritual agents from the very headquarters of evil" (Ephesians 6:12, J.B. Phillips). This unseen power is a person, whose method of operation can be described as schemes, cunning, wiles, methods of attack, devices, stratagems, and tricks.

Years ago the story flew around the Karen mountains: "When Christians are baptized, they are held under the water until they die. Then three days later they come to life again." People believed the first part readily enough, but could you be sure of the resurrection part? It was put to the test when the first group of Pwo Karen believers and their families gathered along a roadside where the flooded river made a natural baptismal pool. Buoy Gee was first. He gave his testimony boldly, and then went under the baptismal waters. I expect he was rather fearful himself, for he had never seen a baptism — what if the missionaries had deceived him? There were sighs of relief and a ripple almost of amusement when he arose, alive, from the water. The bystanders were now convinced that baptism does not mean literal death, but there was no recalling the rumor that had circled the hills.

"There is a big ogre in the foreigners' country. White people steal children and feed them to the ogre." This had gone the rounds too. It was reported that some Christians closed their eyes to pray before eating, and during that instant a Karen child disappeared. No one could identify the missing child, or give the name of the family, but that it had happened was indisputable. When Christian teenager Du Buey went off to Bible School, it was said that the "ogre" had demolished her. Du Buey came home several times between her school terms, very much alive, but the hill folk still "know" she has been eaten.

When missionaries went on furlough, rumors to explain their absence would be circulated. One couple, it was said, had been killed in a plane crash. Some others had been led away, handcuffed, by the police. Another missionary had grown large buffalo horns on her head and couldn't get through a door. The reappearance of the missionaries should, one would think, give the lie to these stories, but it does not. "Missionaries steal children," says a Karen mother to her little one. When the missionary hears this it is hard not to react in anger. "Christians are cannibals," is another readily believed tale. We are tempted to feel exasperated at their gullibility, for there is, seemingly, nothing too wild or improbable for a Karen to believe.

Behind all these rumors lurks the devil who is the father of lies. It is his strategy to smother the tribal folk under a blanket of fear. If you fear the missionary, you are less likely to believe his message. "Missionaries ship people to the States to be soldiers." This kind of thing needs to be fought by someone on his knees, and the falsity of such stories proved through truth proclaimed and lived out day by day.

We should not be surprised if Satan fosters the illusion that animists are merely uninformed people and that a spot of teaching is all they require. The more he can cover his tracks the better he will be pleased, for no one is going to pray against him if they don't know he is there. If he can be considered as a good joke, or a legendary figure with horns, he can pursue his activities unmolested. The Scriptures, our only firm basis for belief, forthrightly name him as "the evil one", or "the wicked one", and identify him as a person with superhuman powers, with agents who do his will.

It is in this realm that the tribal Christians live. Sometimes we wish we could lift them right out of all such pervasive influences, out of earshot of the voices calling for a return to the old way of life. But this is impossible. There is no physical place beyond Satan's wiles. To change geographical location would merely change the kind of influence he wields. No, it is in the familiar place with all its darkness that the power of the Lord Jesus is to be demonstrated. It is there that the believer will prove, to his own growing wonder and to the amazement of his neighbors, that God is real, near at hand and active in everyday concerns.

The missionary shares the tribal lot and lives in this same atmosphere of compelling evil. We ourselves never lived in a heathen village, only in Christian Lahu villages. We visited heathen Lahu areas but did not stay there. As I have talked with fellow missionaries, and particularly those working with the Karen, I sensed again the darkness and utter bondage of spiritism. Both missionaries and tribal believers live in the midst of it, day after day, night after night. I long for a new band of praying people to share in this spiritual struggle. How essential it is that the missionary knows how to face attacks in the spirit realm, and to be continually strong in the Lord so he can truly help the new "babes in Christ."

The Akha villagers of Kha Yeh had warmly welcomed Peter and Jean Nightingale to live among them. But the headman, when approached for his permission, said: "The spirits say you cannot live inside the village, or even just inside the gate. You are Jesus people with a different religion." And he added magnanimously: "You can build on the ridge over yonder if you like, but you can't live inside the gate." This demon gate with its fertility symbols is renewed annually at New Year. It is more than an approach to the village, for it signifies that those within the gate are under the protection of the spirits. From that time on, no Christian Akha has been allowed to live within the demon gates. Christians have had to move out, and start their own Christian communities. The first two Akha families to become Christians moved to a new area with YaJu, the Akha musician, and his wife Mee Chu and the Nightingale family to form a new village. As the new Christians left their old home, the villagers said the demons were so angered that no baby boys would be born in the new village, and any girls born would be puny. That very year all four Christian families had a baby boy, and what is more they were fat and flourishing!

A few months after this refusal Peter Nightingale had a meeting with the demon priest from Kha Yeh. He had previously challenged this man, old Grandfather Bent Nose: "God's Word says the demons you worship know the Lord Jesus and they fear him as their conqueror. Ask the demons yourself. I challenge you in Jesus' name." Now the reply came, as the old demon priest looked Peter right in the eye and said: "I asked them and they answered 'yes'."

Many years ago Martin Luther affirmed:

"Though this world with devils filled
Should threaten to undo us,
We will not fear, for God has willed
His truth to triumph through us.
The prince of darkness grim, we tremble not for him.
His rage we can endure, for lo, his doom is sure,
One little word shall fell him."

This is what we believe, but even as I write it I am reminded that to be strong in the Lord is never automatic. Being a missionary does not ensure that we will not tremble before the "ancient foe", as Luther called him in that same hymn. I need repeatedly to put on God's complete armor that can resist all the devil's methods of attack. I will not drift into having truth for a belt and righteousness for a breastplate; I must decisively and continually take up this armor. When my hand grows weary in wielding the sword of the Spirit I must make sure that He strengthens my grip. The shield of faith won't just fall into my hands. A lazy, casual head knowledge of the truth will not quench the burning missiles hurled by the ancient foe. But when I am spiritually alert, the Lord can make His truth to triumph even through me.

Chapter 14

Delayed Harvest

"IT IS LIKE going with a lighted match in your hand," wrote Neville Long about pioneering among the Lahu, "but things are damp through and through." After another typical trek he reported, "There is no conviction of sin and we are praying for this, as only the Spirit can do that work."

Pioneers often have only discouraging news to report. There may be friendliness but little spiritual response. Jim and Louise Morris wrote after visiting Karen villages: "We felt we were more tolerated than welcomed." Later they found an increasing attitude of: "Oh, we have heard all that before." Their two carriers, who had seemed on the verge of genuine faith, became cynical and argumentative.

At the beginning missionaries expect these negative reactions but, as time goes on and apathy is as dreary as ever, it is harder to go out with hope in your heart. That little match you carry seems to give a poor light, and it sometimes flickers and almost goes out.

In the North Thailand areas where OMF missionaries have worked, progress has been slow. Hearing of mass movements in India or hundreds of baptisms in South America we rejoice almost enviously, for we have not, as yet, seen such a widespread work of God's Spirit. However, the Lord has had good things to teach us as we have waited on Him. There are the Shan, for example.

The Shan are not a mountain people, nor tribal, being related to the Thai. As well as in a big area of Burma, they live in Thailand in a large pocket along the border north and west of Chiang Mai, covering about 120 square miles. The first spasmodic missionary visits were made way back in 1952, and it was a couple of years later that the first missionary took up residence in a Shan village. The people were friendly, and after a time one or two professed faith in the Lord. But immediately the crushing social pressure of a people proud of their ancient religion, Buddhism, was applied. And the "converts" were indeed crushed, or to change the figure they simply melted away. Over and over again this pattern was repeated. Missionary hopes would be raised as they met people wanting an answer to their spiritual needs, and then suddenly the interest would be extinguished. Some were actually baptized but they too were soon silenced. No violence was needed — the neighborhood unitedly frowned and scolded and scorned until the "convert" repented of his folly in forsaking the ways of the fathers.

Poring over the old records, I found the names of at least sixty Shan people who had professed to believe. That means that sixty times some missionary rejoiced and prayed and taught, and then with a sad heart saw those who had seemed so hopeful turn away. There is a special relationship with someone you have introduced to Christ, and the longer the relationship has had to grow the deeper the sense of loss when the friendship ceases. If it were just a matter of friendship, that could be borne. But when eternal issues are involved the sorrow is doubled. In all this time only a handful of Shan have "lasted" more than ten years.

Over the years missionaries have tried every possible approach. They visited homes and gave out tracts to any who could read. They had children's meetings, but the parents saw to it that the interest didn't develop into anything serious. Young people were encouraged to visit freely. Medical work opened many homes and created goodwill all round. In one town evening meetings were held in seven different homes; but some folk resisted the message, others listened in order to make merit, and none seemed to be really seeking the truth. The New Testament was translated and cassettes made. On furlough in England, Dr. and Mrs. Webb learned about pottery so that they could help the poverty-stricken leprosy patients find a new way of making a living.

Another idea has been to show a series of filmstrips in people's homes, to which the neighbors all gather. Interest may be sustained through the third set, but by the fourth or fifth people are realizing that believing involves a cost, and do not want to see any more.

When we visited Don and Martha Wilson in their small Shan village, there had been an epidemic amongst the water buffalo and many animals had died. The spirit priest had ordered demon strings tied across every gate of every yard in the village. To reach the Wilson's house, we had to walk under one with its little baubles hanging from it, for they shared a yard with other families who had hastened to comply with the order. As we strolled around the village in the afternoon people were friendly enough, but everywhere were demon strings, symbols of united village action. What would it be like for a lone Christian family unwilling, for the Lord's sake, to tie a string across the gate?

A fine young Christian Thai girl joined the team as a fellow worker. Pitsamai entered into the missionary yearnings and disappointments, for she too came home after visiting Shan families and said: "They are friendly and seem to want me to visit, but there is a stolid indifference to the message." Missionary Lotte Fehlmann found a sort of wry comfort in this. For years she had fussed, wondering after a round of visits with only blankness for a response, whether it was because she was a foreigner. Was it because she made mistakes in the language? Did they understand what she said? Had she been unable to establish rapport? But here was Pitsamai, certainly not a foreigner, speaking the language, understanding the cultural background, liked by people, and yet still meeting that wall of indifference.

The missionaries themselves have prayed, and so have their prayer partners. For two years the

North Thailand missionary team concentrated prayer on the Shan, asking the Lord to enter the scene and show His power to save and keep His own. Now, some thirty years after that initial telling of the Good News, there is at last a small group whose lives give evidence that God is answering prayer.

But what of our reactions during the months and years when our prayers appeared to be unanswered? This struggle has not been confined to Shan missionaries, for all of us at some time have had to suffer the discipline of patience, when the work seemed so slow. What is the proper response to that discipline?

There is a place for us to examine ourselves in God's presence. "Am I the hindrance to God's working? Do I have wrong attitudes that prevent God from answering prayer? Am I operating under my own steam, or do I walk in the power of the Spirit? Have I prayed enough? Do I love the people or am I exasperated with them for being so slow to respond?" God responds faithfully to such honest evaluation. But it is easy to slip into self-questioning guilt. Then the enemy-prompted questions do not lead us to seek God's remedy, but rather immerse us in guilt and self-preoccupation. Dwelling on my deficiencies and failures will keep me firmly settled at the bottom of the Slough of Despond. Being a habitué of that unpleasant spot, I know whereof I write!

We must be honest before God; we must also be honest in our reports of the work. This is not easy.

Should we paint the picture as black as we see it —
and run the risk of appearing to be missionary
failures, lacking in faith? Should we pick out the
most current bit of encouragement and focus on
that? But that does not show the true state of
affairs. Never to yield either to undue pessimism
or undue optimism requires good balance, and not
all of us can continually maintain that posture.

Discouragement can lead in one of two directions. It can lead down to a dogged hanging on
without any hope that things will be better. Even
to read the record of years of delay and disappointment does something to your spirit. To
live through them with hope deferred making the
heart sick opens the door to a low state of
expectancy that is really cynicism. In all our tribal
areas we have seen people who seemed to begin
well but in course of time turned back to the old
ways. So it is easy to drift into a negative attitude
that stifles faith. Perhaps this sin is easier for
older, experienced missionaries. The newly-
arrived missionary is full of faith and idealism, and
views new converts with an optimism that is fed by
faith in the God of the impossible. But we oldsters
wonder if we should wait to rejoice until we see if
their faith is genuine, instead of happily trusting
God to complete what He has begun. This is
subtle and it is sinful, for it allows faith to be
molded by our experience rather than by the
promises of God.

Discouraging things need not discourage us.
Discouragement can also be a path leading

upwards, for it can tell us in loudest tones that we need the Lord. A much-loved teacher at Prairie Bible Institute used to say: "Don't be hopeless. Just be helpless." If we view our helplessness properly and don't just complain about it, God can move in strength. We can exhort and teach, but we can't force people to believe and grow. We can pray and take our stand against the enemy who hinders and binds, but it is God who sets men free. To be aware of my inability to help people is one of God's blessings, for it can take me immediately to the one who has this ability.

Of course Lotte and her fellow worker Judy Crossman have known times of discouragement. But always there has been the stabilizing sense that God has called them to witness to the Shan, so it must be His purpose to build a church amongst them. On several occasions the Field Council wondered if the team should be moved to a more fruitful area, but God never relieved these ladies of their burden for the Shan, and kept their faith kindled. Today they have the joy of caring for some Shan believers, most of them literate and all keen to learn the Word. Two of the group used to be opium addicts, but today their lives are wonderfully changed. And they are all constantly sharing the Gospel with neighbors and relatives.

Even through discouraging days the Lord gave them encouragements. One was a Shan teenager named Lanna, in the town of Khunyuam. Her parents, wanting her to have a good education, sent her away to the larger town of Maesariang, about halfway along the motor road between her home and Chiang Mai. The Christian hostel seemed a safe place for a young teenage girl to board. But it wasn't safe as far as Gospel influences were concerned, and Lanna's interest grew until at a youth camp, when she was fifteen, she received the Lord and later was baptized. When she came home on holidays she spent a lot of time with the Webbs who had the great joy of sharing the Word with her. She grew as a Christian and gave great promise for the future.

At the age of seventeen Lanna went to Chiang Mai to teachers training college. Back in Khunyuam a young fellow was showing interest in her, but she was not interested in his overtures. On her first term break she went home and one afternoon, carefully choosing the time when her family were out in their ricefields, the young man went to her house. He locked the doors on the inside, shot and killed Lanna and then turned the gun on himself. For Lanna it meant a swift entry to her heavenly home, safe from the persecution that would undoubtedly have come to her as an adult in the Shan community. For her family and the whole village it was tragedy.

The double funeral was, perforce, a heathen one. Lanna's mother, though herself not believing, knew Lanna would want a Christian funeral and asked the Webbs and Lotte to go over to the house. But it was impossible, for the demon ceremonies were already in full swing. For Lanna's mother the only comfort was that Lanna's face was peaceful and happy, even in death. All the neighbors remarked on this fact. The general belief is that the spirit of the one who dies a violent death must come back to its home and trouble the family. But they said Lanna's spirit never bothered them, and her mother also had a dream in which she saw Lanna, who said she was happy and told her mother not to be upset.

Another encouragement was Grandfather Saen. The Webbs first went to his village to visit leprosy patients, and found he had TB. He was in his late 70s and widely respected, so that when he believed no one opposed him, and he was a Christian for about two years before the Lord took him Home. His family, though not themselves believing, were concerned that his funeral be fully Christian, so they asked the missionaries to plan it all. One of the Christian men helped with formalities like consulting the village elders about the burial place and making the coffin. A team of Bible School students who were there at the time helped collect flowers to decorate the coffin, and then all joined in for a great day of witness, with a message and plenty of singing at the house, and more singing at the grave. The family begged the Christians to return in the evening so as to prevent neighbors coming to cheer them up with drinking and gambling — they knew that Grandfather wouldn't have wanted that. So that evening an outdoor evangelistic meeting was held in the yard and many heard the Gospel, including a young relative, Jan Dee, who eventually believed and for a time attended Bible School. That day Jan Dee talked at length with Uncle A and was impressed with answers to his questions.

Who is Uncle A? That really is his name — it is not just a letter of the alphabet. He is another of the bright spots in the Shan work. He was baptized in 1974, when he was in his middle 50s. His wife and children, though not in the least in sympathy, had to take a lot of ridicule from relatives and neighbors, which naturally added to their resentment. He has stood alone, against the rest of the family, who at times said they wished he would leave. It is wearing to live under a cloud of disapproval, and his home life has not been happy, but the Lord has enabled this naturally hot-tempered man to bear patiently with them. One day when he was specially feeling his loneliness he was cheered by passages in Revelation that assured him of the coming day when there will be an end to all tears and trouble. And he was encouraged to believe God for his family, for whom he is deeply concerned.

One day Uncle A's twenty-year-old son was playing with a gun and accidentally shot another village lad. Both families involved are poor so the headman advised them not to go to the police but settle the case themselves. Uncle A agreed to pay the medical expenses, but the other family saw their opportunity to get something extra from the situation, and things were very tense. This was barely settled when his wife became dangerously ill and he cared for her patiently, staying in the hospital with her for two weeks. One missionary who watched Uncle A's reactions through these trials said she was impressed with his loving attitude to his family despite their ill treatment of him, and his quiet faithfulness to the Lord.

We all have our areas of seeming impossibility, and it is in these very areas that God has opportunity to teach us about His power to deal with the impossible. Think of Abraham's faith concerning the birth of a promised son. There is an interesting difference between the King James Version and Revised Version in Romans 4:19. The KJV says: "He considered *not* his own body now dead," but the RV says: "He considered his own body now dead." I expect he did both. He considered — he faced facts, for reality said it was impossible for him to have a child. But he also considered *not* — the natural facts had nothing to do with it. He was not deterred by the impossible, for he was possessed by the conviction that God can perform whatever He has promised.

One of God's promises is that He is building His church. As His children we need this continual conviction. Does the virtue of hope strike you as a pallid, easy virtue? Hope as it is seen in the Scriptures is not the result of an optimistic temperament. There are people who hope vaguely that everything will turn out well in the end, but that is not a God-given expectation. Hope comes directly from Him, nurtured by the Word. I know this to be so, but for me it has not been an uninterrupted experience, for I have not always allowed Him to quicken my hope in His word.

Many of us have found it hard to walk in hope, not only because of our own areas of discouragement but also because of the unmet needs. They are legion, and we cannot be complacent about what we are doing for it stands against what should and could be done if there were more people to help. The areas to be evangelized are so wide, and the villages with believers are scattered so far apart. It is easy to feel overwhelmed, for example, with the translation work still to be done. Such a burden can do one of two things. It can breed a discouraged feeling that the job will *never* be done, or it can send you to your knees.

I have found that the work I don't do tires me more than the work I do. The "undone" becomes such a wearisome burden that I can't rejoice over what has been accomplished. This is true in such mundane areas as housework. I adore lists and always carry around scraps of paper covered with things I intend to do that day, but of course I never get them all done and the thought of that long, uncompleted list wearies me. The needs of the work press in on every side, but it is not God's thought for us to be tired from work we haven't yet accomplished. This is a frustration that robs us of our joy. It has been said of Francis of Assisi and his companions: "They knew, even in their mortal days, even in defeat and pain and fear, the meaning of joy. It was a gift to them, the resurrection gift of Christ who said 'Your heart shall rejoice and your joy no man taketh from you,' but in the thought of Francis to be joyful was also a command, as much so as the command to be poor and humble and to walk in love. It was their business to see that their joy was not taken from them. It was a flame to be tended and if it went out, to be immediately lit again. He knew there was no better armor against sin than joy."[1]

I am surrounded by needs, but God has not appointed me to meet *all* of them. He has given responsibilities that I must fulfill if I am to walk in obedience. The Lord Jesus said He delighted to do the will of God, and it is God's purpose for me to delight in doing my appointed work. I am not to be depressed about duty that is not mine to assume. Even in such a solemn matter as meeting spiritual needs, I must distinguish between the people *I* want to help and the people *God* wants me to help. He desires to renew our faith so that we continually rejoice in hope.

---

[1] *My God and My All* by Elisabeth Goudge.

Chapter 15

Does It Work?

IT IS ALWAYS a day of rejoicing when a tribesman says he wants to believe in the Lord Jesus and to burn his demon things. He prays and commits himself to the Lord. Would you then count him as a Christian, the possessor of eternal life? Few of our tribal missionaries would. Experience has taught us that this act generally means he is fed up with sacrificing pigs and chickens to the demons, and is now ready to see if Christianity works any better.

The tribesman feels helpless before the caprice of the weather — too much rain and the rice rots, or not enough rain and consequent drought. He has no way of coping with plagues of rats. He has little defense against sickness and death. The only way open to him is that of placating the spirits that in his view control these things. He's not thinking about sin, but just wants to survive disaster.

It's not strange then that very few, if any, of the tribal people have trusted God at their first hearing of the Gospel. Most people in so-called Christian countries have had some exposure to Christian teaching, but the tribal man has no such background. I know of no tribal person whose initial reaction to God's good news was a yearning for Him or a response to His love. They are exactly like us — concerned about their own wants. He doesn't turn away from us because of this, because we are the kind of people who need Him most. It's the selfish people He came to save, and His love is large enough to meet us at the point of need. He patiently helps us to discover that what we wanted all along was relationship with Him.

The missionary speaks of a Person and a relationship with that Person. The tribal man hears these truths, but his needs shape his thinking, and the message he "hears" is not the message that the missionary has given. He "hears" that perhaps this One who is said to have power over evil spirits will shield him from illness and keep him from death. The missionary talks about Jesus stilling the storm, and the winds and waves obeying Him. Surely then He could do something about the rice crops, and the necessity for rain, not too early and not too late? The missionary never for a moment claims that God will keep a believer from all trouble but this is, I think, what the new inquirer "hears."

His prayer of commitment is sincere, but may mean no more than that he is giving God the chance to prove His power. It rarely involves submission or any true sense of sin. Missionaries do, of course, teach about sin and repentance, but the tribesman is concerned with sickness and natural calamity. He doesn't see himself in the presence of a holy God, but just wants someone who will control the ills of life. And our God is compassionate. He meets the man at his point of need.

Paul talks about the Thessalonian church that turned *to* God *from* idols. Of course the "turning from" and "turning to" should be simultaneous, but when the tribesman "believes" the only thing that is clear to the missionary is that he has "turned from" the demons. This tremendous first step does free him to be taught by the Lord, and a relationship with the Lord is now possible. But it is not clear at this point whether he has "turned to" the Lord and really seen Him as a Savior from sin. Some of the believers have themselves testified that they did not receive eternal life when they burned their demon paraphernalia. But in this way they showed themselves willing to be taught, and the Lord brought them gradually into full assurance of faith.

God's dealings are suited to each individual's need. He doesn't run us all through the same mill. However, there are some basic lessons He wants us all to learn, and we can observe in His dealings with His tribal children lessons designed to teach them of His power and His love and His holiness.

We see many instances of clear answers to specific prayers. A number of Hmong had confessed Christ in baptism, including Simon. Shortly after this, Simon's wife visited her unbelieving relatives in a distant village and told them what Simon had done. They were furious and said she could not return to him, and if she attempted to get away they would shoot her, for she'd be better off dead than living with a Christian. Meanwhile Simon, just a new believer himself, was anxious about her. Telling no one about it, he decided to spend the whole day quietly alone praying. He "arranged" it with the Lord that she would get safely away and that in the evening they would have a praise meeting with the missionaries. Next morning it "happened" that his wife's parents were both out of the house, and she was away down the trail before anyone realized she had gone. So according to Simon's "arrangement" and by God's power to "arrange", she reached home safely. Simon could hardly contain himself as he told the missionaries of this wonderful answer to prayer, and they did indeed sit down together and have a praise meeting! To Simon it was such loving proof that God knew about him and his wife, cared about what happened to them and was able to free them from the designs of those who opposed them.

After the birth of their first baby the mother was unwell and steadily losing strength. At Simon's suggestion, missionaries and believers gathered together to pray for her. One of the men prayed specifically that the Lord would heal her within three days, and in those three days she improved so dramatically that no one could doubt this answer to prayer. God really did know about them and had heard their cries for help.

When direct answer to prayer was needed, that was what God gave. So when Brother Six was a new believer, two of his newly purchased water buffalo were lost in the forest, and Brother Six and the other Yao believers prayed earnestly that they would be found. They were, and there was great rejoicing. A year and a half later Brother Six and his wife went on a preaching tour to the Yao in Laos, and after they returned two valuable oxen were stolen. Again they prayed, but this time the animals were not recovered. Brother Six was becoming acquainted with his new Lord, and was kept at peace through his loss.

A group of new Lisu believers had experienced many answers to prayer about everyday living, and were learning that God was concerned about the small things. Knowing the miseries of trekking in the rain, they had taken to praying for their missionary, Fiona Lindsay, when she had lengthy trips to make. Even in the rainy season they prayed for dry weather and God answered. One day one of the Christians said to Fiona, "We are always going to pray for dry weather whenever you travel." This was an opportunity to share something more of the Lord's ways, and Fiona took it. "Supposing I am on the trail when your rice crops need rain," she said, "then how will you pray?" It was a totally new thought for them that when God listened to their prayers He also had to remember the needs of others, and was the beginning of the lesson that prayer involves submission to the will of God — though the Lisu might not have stated it in those theological terms.

Those first answers to prayer help the new believers to see that God is really present in His universe, is interested in their affairs and moves to bring them relief from distress. But they must also learn, as we all must, that God cannot be manipulated. He is not placated by offerings of pigs and chickens. He is not like the spirits that acted when the correct ceremonies were performed. He is the almighty God, who is equally able to spare His children from all trial or sustain them through all trial. His loving wisdom dictates which it shall be. And God began to trust His new children to learn this lesson.

Baby Ruth had had a lot of sickness in her seven short months of life, and the day came when her father Job, one of the earliest Hmong believers, could see that she was not going to recover. He pleaded with the Lord to restore her, and in a sense bargained with God, saying he would go everywhere preaching God's good news to his fellow Hmong if healing was granted. But missionary Don Rulison, seeing the need to help them face the possibility of the child's death, asked Job's wife if she would still believe in the Lord Jesus, even if her baby should die. She replied that she would still believe. And she did. The sorrowing parents were able to make a complete break with all the demon ceremonies required for a heathen funeral. When the women started to wail, old Granny admonished them not to cry as if they had no hope. Don overheard Job reassuring another small daughter that baby Ruth had gone on ahead of them to be with the Lord. In the songs of hope that were sung and the Word that was read at home and at the graveside, the Lord drew near to them. Job carved a small cross, which not only served to mark the site but represented victory, not the victory of God's healing but of His power to comfort His children.

The animist fears death, which is seen to be the work of an evil spirit, showing his displeasure. But when Noah's small daughter, "Good News", died the Lord comforted the family with the certainty that they would meet her again. Noah said, "We cry because we miss her, but we believe and trust the Lord. Now I must never turn from Him or I won't see Good News again." The knowledge that his child was already in the Lord's presence was a new hope and incentive to follow Him along the narrow way that leads to life.

The Dunns' story shows the way in which God gradually reveals Himself to those who seek Him. When Mrs. Dunn was just a teenager she was sitting quietly at her embroidery work one day when suddenly a snake fell from the roof into her lap. It didn't harm her but it was a frightening omen, for everybody in her Hmong village knew that she, or her children, would die prematurely. When she married and lost her first two babies, it was obvious that the deaths were a fulfillment of that sign. Then she herself became very ill with a kidney condition. All the usual demon ceremonies were tried with no success and finally, though the clan was loath to lose two such good workers, it was agreed that the only thing left was to try the Christian way. The Dunns had been very friendly with missionary Leona Bair, and open to what she shared of the Gospel, so they were prepared to burn their demon things and find out if the Lord could really help them. The night before the decision, Mrs. Dunn looked out and saw Leona's house filled with a heavenly light, and this was a sign to her that it was right to believe. She had been distressed, unable to sleep and afraid of dying, and one of the first proofs of God's care was the gift of refreshing sleep. She said the Lord was bringing light into her heart and she was able to rest, knowing that she was now in His keeping.

The Dunns, now in their middle thirties, had been Christians for about a year when twins were safely born. But Mrs. Dunn went into shock. The placenta had not been delivered and she was hemorrhaging badly. The normal Hmong procedure would have been to do demon worship, and the relatives urged Mr. Dunn to do this, but he didn't panic — he prayed. A Christian woman came along to help and the condition was remedied. In fact, all the Christians rallied round, taking time off work to be with the Dunns and encourage them.

The twins flourished at first but then began to have convulsions, which is a frightening business for parents even if you don't attribute it to demon powers. Although the Dunns were truly believing, old thought patterns persist. Their fields were near some cliffs where, everyone said, lived a lot of demons, and the twins had been near them. Was this exposure to the spirits the reason for the convulsions? And there was another troubling thing. One of the little girls didn't seem to like her mother, the other objected to her father. As all Hmong know, this means that the child's spirit has already rejected the family and is going to seek relief in death.

When the twins were two and a half they became ill with what their parents thought must be measles. They were blotchy red and badly swollen, so the Dunns took them to Chiang Mai hospital. Even so, the first twin died. Then the neighbors urged the parents to perform the demon ceremony of cutting the twins' spirits apart so the second one would not die. It must have been a real temptation for the anxious parents, but they did not give in, even though there were some stabbing doubts about the wisdom of their decision. Were they denying their baby something that would help her? Then the second twin died and was brought home. Old Granny in her grief struck at the small body crying out: 'You didn't want to stay with us. Why did you come and then leave us? Why didn't you like us?" The non-Christians didn't bother to sympathize with people who were so unfeeling as to sit idle and let their children die.

Again the Christians loved and helped them and the missionary grieved with them. But it was Simon, now an established believer, who was really able to minister to them. His mother had just died from cancer and his much-loved small daughter had disappeared, probably drowned in a flooded river. He could most truly enter into their sorrow. He sent them a cassette saying, "I've just lost two of my family so I know how you feel. I can't help your hearts in the way you want help just now. I can't bring your babies back to you. But remember they have gone ahead of you and you will meet them. Don't be lost in your grief. Don't put all your energy into sorrow but trust the Lord. Ask Him to increase your faith. Set your heart wholly on Him." This was far more help to them than any missionary words could ever be. We have never been tempted to seek the spirits' help in sickness. But a Hmong could fully enter into their loss, and Hmong words carried weight. And so they were comforted, and leaned the more heavily on the Lord.

The Dunns had always been responsive as Leona shared the Word with them. The Lord had met with them in sorrow, and they were committed to His way. Yet there was something lacking. The Lord knows when we need new truth, and when we are ready for new growth, new steps. He took Mr. Dunn to a leaders' conference, and during those days the bits and pieces of truth that Mr. Dunn had grasped fell into place. They were no longer unconnected statements, but took form and were embodied in the Lord Jesus. The doctrines he had accepted, hoping they were true, really were. Now he entered a new relationship with a Person, and there has been a difference in his life since. Each time we see something more of the Lord we are changed; and our faith grows as we prove that He is totally trustworthy.

We were often perplexed in our own praying for the new believers. We knew that death, illness or accident would be interpreted as demons' vengeance. It would take time for the new believers to learn they were not at the mercy of the spirits, and we felt fearful that they would be turned away by the first trials. On a natural plane such fears were not unreasonable. We had seen it many times, in people like Ying. He was such a promising young man, who had visited the two Barbaras' village often and had learned to read even before deciding to become a Christian. After he, his wife and his elderly father burned their demon things, a few others in the village took the same step, and Ying started literacy classes for them. Then his baby died, and five days later his wife, overwhelmed with grief, turned back. Then the old father died and that was the final blow. Ying and his wife reshouldered the old burden of the demon ways. This is a sorrow that never grows any less with repetitions, and with such memories as these it seemed difficult to know what to ask for the new believers.

We know assuredly that God has power to guard His faltering children. He can give protection in danger and change the natural course of events. Even as the new believers' first prayers were requests for safety and good health, we were sometimes tempted to ask for these very things for them. But the truth of God's power cannot be separated from His wisdom, His love and His holiness. He has unlimited concern for His own. He uses circumstances so that we will learn of Him, and shapes events so that we will know and use His grace which is never in short supply. Our natural impulse to ask for shelter for the new believers had to yield to prayers for their highest good. "Lord, give these babes the signs of Your Power that would most help them to experience Your love."

In teaching the new believers that He cannot be manipulated He also taught us that He can be trusted. We were not to be dismayed at what He allowed. Standing against Satan's schemes, we were to allow God to be God.

We were concerned not only for the new believers but for all the unbelieving neighbors who were watching to see what would happen to anyone who defied the spirits. These fears had to be given over to Him. He did not need us to be careful of His reputation. We sometimes acted as though we thought He did not know the best way or time to show His power. We were also wrong in assuming that if God intervened miraculously the neighbors too would believe. The fifteen-year-old son of a believing Lisu widow was considering becoming a Christian, and one day he wrote out in Lisu on a piece of paper, "Number Four Son (his name) really believes in Jesus." It was as though he wanted to make a record of the transaction. Then he hid the paper in the bamboo wall. Shortly afterward he was racked with terrible tetanus-like spasms. Anxious to do what they could to help, the neighbors quickly did some spirit ceremonies, but the pain continued. Finally they carried him over to the house of one of the Lisu believers, who prayed and the spasms ceased. Even people in the village acknowledged that though the demons were angry, Jesus had power over them. One would have thought this would have convinced the onlookers that they needed such a God. But this does not automatically follow. On one occasion Christian Hmong had moved into a Hmong village and had just finished building their houses when a whirlwind swept through the village and blew off all the roofs except those of the Christians. The non-Christians all agreed that the Lord had taken care of His children, but no one was moved to believe in Him.

We learned to trust God's ways with new believers. I think of little Widow Sing's experience. She was an enthusiastic member of the Scheuzgers' literacy class but she couldn't wait for organized lessons. In fact she made a positive nuisance of herself, always turning up at the house at awkward moments, just when Adri was putting the children to bed or when her arms were covered with flour. On the rare occasions when the house was empty of visitors and the missionary family was hoping to put their feet up for a moment, you could count on it that a determined little widow, her glasses perched on the end of her nose, would push in at the door and ask, "What is this word?" She often exhausted their patience but they rejoiced with her when she learned to read and was able to find spiritual food in the Word.

After Widow Sing became a Christian her daughter Ku also believed, was baptized and appeared to be following the Lord. She was of marriageable age but there were no Christian fellows suitable for her to marry. The village took things into their own hands and, unknown to Widow Sing but with Ku's consent, arranged a typical Hmong "wedding kidnapping." Ku was taken off in the night to become the second wife in a wealthy heathen home. From the villagers' standpoint she had made a good match, but her mother grieved over her and another sorrow was soon to come, for Ku died giving birth to her first baby. The widow did not even have the solace of knowing that Ku had repented of her ways. But the Lord ministered to her and, as one missionary commented, "She was visibly sustained." People could see that something (they didn't know it was Someone) was enabling her to face the ills of life. She was finding her strength in the Word, and the neighbors were able to see one who manifested the grace of God.

In our anxiety for God's glory, we sometimes forget that He will take care of it. We fear His name will be blackened before an unbelieving world, and that weak Christians will be offended and turn away. We need to remember that Christ knew what it was to have followers turn aside. He is the one who truly knows how to nurture the church.

Chapter 16

No Instant Christians

"**P**LEASE PRAY FOR two of the local elders who seem unconcerned about discipline in the church," read one prayer request. "They themselves don't always bother to come to services and they are not always completely honest in business." Other missionaries wrote: "Please pray for the G's. They moved to another area, taking their few possessions with them, plus the church funds." "Pray for the Christian headman who, at a funeral for a non-Christian, took part in some of the heathen ceremonies."

Being a parent is a very rewarding experience. But alongside the delights of watching individuality and character grow, parents also have to cope with colicky and teething infants, fretful days and disturbed nights. Spiritual parenthood too combines both experiences. There is great joy at seeing your tribal friends born into the family of God, and it is a high privilege to have these "babes in Christ" to care for, cheered by their growth and their first faltering steps of faith. But they too have "teething pains", giving broken nights and anxious days. And the fact is that while God is teaching the new believers to walk, teaching them that He can be trusted, He is also teaching missionaries to be responsible "parents." The only way to learn to bring up children is to bring up children. So God conducts dual teaching sessions, on-the-job training.

One of the most difficult aspects of bringing up children is to know the standard of behavior suitable for their varying ages. This is a missionary problem too, especially since missionaries are prone to be idealists with unrealistic standards for new believers. We know that learning to walk is an up-and-down business. The infant falls a lot at first and when he takes off on his own he bumps into things. No one blames him for this flawed performance — he is doing fine according to his growth. In spiritual parenting the first stumbles and falls are harder to accept. It is right to be concerned about sin, for our longing for the new Christians is full conformity to Christ. But very few follow undeviatingly along the path that leads to this. Stumbling seems to be part of the process.

The prayer requests at the beginning of this chapter were answered. For many years the two elders have been faithful men of God walking in faith and obedience. The G's eventually returned, along with their possessions and the church funds. And the Christian headman separated himself from old demon practices and turned whole-heartedly to the Lord. We now know the answers to those prayers, but at the time missionaries could not help but be anxious. Is this kind of anxiety wrong? Loving concern for those in our care can grow into the worry that God pronounces to be sin. When we wish for "instant Christians", not making allowance for the time lapse in growth, we are well on our way to that sinful anxiety. We rightfully grieve over early stumbles and falls, but we will grieve unduly if we forget that many years go into the growth of a strong tree. We don't want weeds that pop up overnight.

Satan can take advantage of this situation, seeing to it that the missionary feels guilty about the new believers' lapses or responsible that his teaching is not more effective. More serious still, we may feel that somehow the Lord has let us down and failed to show His power. This kills trust in God's sure purpose for His family. The perfecting of the Body of Christ is His avowed intent, but we may lose sight of this fact and send up a lot of worry prayers.

One difficulty in judging standards of behavior appropriate to growth is our ignorance of the local "measuring cups." For example, missionaries sometimes complain at the slowness with which tribal people learn the importance of gathering together for worship and teaching. To us this looks like lack of appetite for the things of God. It may be that. But it certainly reflects the fact that in the tribal culture there is no worship service on Sunday, nor Bible study on Wednesday. They do have special times for demon ceremonies, as at New Year, and some ceremonial days are prompted by a particular need. When someone is ill the Lahu will have two or three nights of demon dancing. But to go at a set time on a set day every week to sit quietly and study takes getting used to. Then, just when you think the habit has been learned, all the Christians depart to their field houses to get on with their weeding. This may be many hours walk away so it is difficult to come home for Sundays. How can you teach people that aren't there? I remember watching a mother hen who had hatched a nestful of baby ducks. All went well until the ducks swam off into the stream, when the frantic mother flew up and down along the bank, trying to help those unprotected babies. But they were out of reach. Missionaries know this kind of trial.

A Christian friend of ours had a responsible position which included handling money. He was besieged by needy relatives wanting to borrow, and he was too kind-hearted to refuse. Eventually there was a scandal over missing funds, which was a great pity for it began with someone wanting to be obliging — no dishonesty was intended. This kind of thing is not unknown in tribal villages where there have never been bank statements or auditors or written agreements. Just as parents have to sort out the reason for a child breaking something valuable — was it just childish awkwardness, or an act of defiance? — part of spiritual parenting is trying to understand the tribal values and sort out the difference between deliberate dishonesty and the following of cultural ways.

Doe Jones tells of her perplexity at the time of the first Christian funeral in her Hmong village. She was still learning the language and the culture and had no idea about the significance of the Hmong burial ceremonies, which are detailed and scrupulously observed. The Christians themselves weren't sure what was custom and what was spirit involvement, and they kept questioning Doe.

"Is it all right to put a woman's jacket on the man who has died?" When Doe queried the reason for this she was told it was for convenience. The women's jackets have a large collar which makes it easier to carry the body without touching the head. That sounded reasonable, and Doe told them to go ahead. Later she discovered that this custom, and other things that were done, *did* have demon significance. But she was anxious to avoid imposing foreign burial customs on the new Christians, so she kept saying that they should do as they thought best. It was very distressing. The Christians felt helpless, and so did Doe. The heathen were scornful because the Christians "didn't have any ritual."

In both kinds of parenting, it is hard to let go your toddler's hand and allow him to have a few spills. We know their inexperience so we coddle them too long, or else in our zeal for their growth we may thrust them prematurely into situations they cannot manage. Holding on too long deprives them of their learning experience. A father became impatient with his nine year old and did for her what it was taking her too long to do. When the mother asked her tearful daughter what was wrong, she said, "Daddy acts like I am not here." Most of us have made some mistakes along this line, insensitively taking over as if the tribal believer wasn't there. There have been grounds for the accusation of missionary paternalism, but it is hard to know at what stages to give increasing independence. The distracted parents of any teenager will tell you how difficult it is.

Along with the discouraging stumbles and our own inefficiency as spiritual parents, there are encouragements too. Stressing problems leads us to prayer, but we need also to stress victories that lead us to rejoice. One who some years ago could hardly pull himself away from gambling to come to the evening service has now been to Bible School and is effectively serving the Lord. An early encouragement among the Yao was in the matter of money. At a Christmas feast the new believers gave gifts for the Lord's work. Then Brother Six sold a pig and gave all the money to the Lord, because the pig had once been sick and the Lord healed it in answer to prayer. As others gave too, a church fund came into being with a treasurer to care for it. Later the Yao had their new rice festival when the first fruits of their crop were brought to the church as a token of thanks to the Lord. In view of the fact that the Yao are good businessmen and not easily parted from their money, their giving signified spiritual growth.

The growth process also includes learning to pray for other people's needs. One missionary was encouraged by Mr. Grey's prayer, "reaching out as far as Jonah's sick wife, a missionary's trip home, and the two families newly believing up north — rather than the usual 'Lord, heal my son's cold'." It was not wrong to pray about the cold, but God has interests beyond health and wants to involve us in them. So in the early Hmong days missionaries rejoiced to hear Noah, Job and Widow Sing praying fervently for the salvation of their neighbors. And it was an encouragement for the Yao missionaries to hear Brother Six praying for them by name.

In the pioneer days the missionary with his lack of forest and agricultural skills seemed a strange and helpless creature to the tribal people. All Hmong children help to gather firewood and girls grow up expecting to trim trees after they have been chopped, and bring the wood to the village. They couldn't understand how difficult this work seemed to the lady missionaries, especially those that hailed from the city. The Hmong themselves are very independent and take pride in being able to fend for themselves. But one Sunday afternoon along the trail to Doe Jones's front door came little Mrs. Ba Ju with two small girls, each carrying a bundle of firewood. Mrs. Ba Ju knew that getting the firewood was a chore for the missionary, and fellowship in the Gospel was enabling her to enter into Doe's trials.

Later, when Doe was living with the Hmong in an area infiltrated by Communists, the Christians decided that all of them, including the missionary, must leave the next morning. Doe couldn't help thinking that if the Reds wanted to get rid of her this would be a convenient night to do it. Just at dusk, along came a young man. "Come to our house to sleep," he said. "It is lonely here. My sister is at home and you can stay with her." Their thoughtfulness left a final happy memory of her stay there.

A Hmong lady was coming home from her fields late one afternoon, and like housewives the world over was wondering what they would have for supper. Passing through a neighbor's garden she noticed some cabbage and thought that this was just what was needed. According to Hmong custom it is correct to pick, in moderation, from a neighbor's field. However there were only a couple of cabbages left, and as she bent to pick one she heard "a voice in her heart" saying: "Don't pick those; there aren't enough for the owners." She recognized the Speaker of those words and obeyed what He said.

Village relationships can be considerably strained if someone's animal gets loose in someone else's fields. Sheeker's buffalo got into Aloo's rice field one day and destroyed part of the crop. Instead of the usual big accusation session Sheeker, a new Lisu believer, said, "We are Christians now. Let's settle this in a Christian way," and he readily paid for the damage done. Being mortal, he couldn't resist pointing out that Aloo's fence was no good. Aloo said he was unable to fix the fence because he had a bad foot, and Sheeker, who was learning to walk the second mile, offered to help fix it. Next day he got together a small work party and the fence was mended. This caused quite a sensation in the village and Sheeker's old father, who was not a

Christian, said that in all his life he had never seen a law case settled so amicably.

Leona Bair had been visiting a Hmong village for teaching and fellowship with some new believers. She could have left on an afternoon bus, but the girls wanted her to stay an extra night. Next morning they left at 3 a.m. to walk the four hours out to the motor road with her, and when she caught her bus they had another four hours walk back. These were small things, certainly, but is it not small evidences that convince us we are loved? The proofs of God's love often come in unspectacular ways, but they warm the heart, and the small kindnesses of God's tribal children were comforting too. In fact, none of the encouragements mentioned in this chapter are showy successes, but they are perhaps more appropriate to growth. If it is true that the longest journey begins with a single step, as the ancient proverb has it, then these single steps *are* important and we may encourage ourselves by remembering that God is in the business of teaching all His children to walk.

Chapter 17

Lord, Give Him Good Dreams

A HMONG ABOUT to go on a journey has a dream in which he sees someone dressed in red or with blood upon him. This is a warning that the trip must be postponed. A Karen plans to begin building a house — but if he has a "bad dream" the night before he knows he has picked the wrong site. Or if he has chosen a place to do his fields and dreams something unsettling, he realizes he has been warned and must change. The tribal folk believe dreams are given so they will know the spirits' wishes. Only a fool would disregard their warnings.

Soon after believing in the Lord, the first Hmong Christians were frightened by an epidemic of dreams of calamity and death. This said to them that the spirits were displeased and were urging them to return to the demon way before judgment should fall. For many years the Hmong had unquestioningly heeded the spirits' warnings, and at the thought of disregarding these dreams they were gripped by fear. For one family it was too shattering, and feeling they must protect themselves they turned from the Lord's way. The night following the decision to become a Christian, or following baptism, is a crucial time when dreams seem doubly important.

I grew up believing that dreams were the aftermath of too much cheese and chocolate. And as for people who tried to interpret dreams and searched for meaning in them, I thought of them as not facing reality and on the verge of fanaticism. So as a young missionary in China I didn't know how to react when people actually believed in the Lord through a vision or a dream. I remember one man who had, as far as I know, no previous contact with the Gospel. In a vivid dream he saw a shining white figure, who told him to find a local gospel hall and believe what he was told there. He obeyed the instruction and received new life in Christ. I had a problem reconciling my opinion on dreams with what actually happened. But I should have seen that the Word has many references to God using dreams for His own purposes. He meets people where they are, and speaks in ways they understand. To the old grannies who will never learn to read His Word for themselves, God speaks even today in other ways. As missionaries we must just accept this.

It is a common experience to be welcomed in a tribal village with the words: "We knew you would come, for we dreamed about your arrival." On one occasion, two Lahu preachers from Thailand were able to go with Larry to visit Lahu villages in Laos — the first time he had ever had Lahu Christian companions in that area. When they arrived in a small Christian village they were expected, for one of the men had had a dream of Larry and two Lahu teachers visiting them. On another occasion a Yao lady dreamed of the Yao missionaries' arrival, so she didn't go to her fields but waited to see them. It is almost as though God sent a telegram to His children preparing them for our coming.

To Christians, God sometimes gives rebuke and guidance via dreams. Akha believer A Meh had been delaying baptism, when for four successive nights he had the same dream. He felt, and rightly, that the Lord was giving him a powerful nudge, and he immediately asked to be baptized. A young Christian, Leng, was being tempted by his brother to join him in looking for girls at night. Premarital sex is the norm for Hmong teenagers, but Leng did have a conscience about it. Then he had a dream of two paths, one wide and one narrow. He went along the narrow one but then looking down he decided to go on the wider path and slithered down the slope to it, only to discover that he was splattered with filth. On waking he understood that to give in to temptation would be to walk on that wider path — unclean in God's sight. For a week he wrestled with this and then two Hmong Christian leaders visiting the village spoke about the truth in 1 John 1:9. The Word clinched the matter and Leng quietly confessed his sin, putting it from him. His load was lifted and he had peace.

When Mr. Gar and his family became Christians, the "family" included two daughters-in-law. Both sets of parents were furious when they heard the news, and came as soon as possible to the village. One daughter-in-law was removed from the dangerous Christian influence and taken back to her parents' home. This was against Hmong custom, for the Gar family had already paid the bride price for her. The second set of parents wanted to do likewise, but their daughter dug in her heels, stating firmly that she was a believer and wasn't going to submit to being taken home. Her parents then angrily demanded the payment of a second bride price. I used to think the bride price was demeaning, as though the wife was a commodity to be sold like a buffalo or pig. But this is not the case. The paying of a price establishes that the marriage is legal and binding. It stabilizes marriage and is a protection for the wife.

Mr. Gar hadn't anticipated that his faith might involve him in family disputes and cost him actual cash, for the Hmong bride price is paid in silver bars. The least possible amount would be the equivalent of US$250, but it could be as high as $800. To forget about being a Christian would be the easy solution, but he wasn't at ease even considering such a step. Finally he went to talk it over with Mark, a quiet, unassuming Hmong church leader whose spiritual advice is much valued. Mark exhorted him to be faithful, but what really convinced him was a dream. In it all the people in his village came to him one by one and said they had been impressed by his believing, but if he chose to go back to demon ways they would make a similar choice. Up to this point Mr. Gar had been considering his own material good, but now he saw that to save himself trouble would involve many others, and put them in spiritual jeopardy. So he chose to follow the Lord though it was costly. In fact this brought blessing to the whole family, for as one of the Barbaras remarked: "In spite of the wrongness of all this the daughter-in-law was worth the double price, for she is a real gem."

The Lord also ministers comfort through dreams and visions. Old Mr. Chieh Shua had been bedridden for years, and towards the end of his life he did seem to trust the Lord, though he was not too clear either in his mind or in his faith. One night he had a vision of the road leading up into heaven and the One who walked upon that road. Next morning he collapsed and was gone, but not before he had shared with his family the things he had seen. It was a comfort both to them and to the missionaries, for it seemed to say that Chieh Shua was now with the Lord whom he had seen in his last hours.

Soo Kan Ya was just a baby when her father became a Christian. Her mother refused to turn to Christ and so Soo Kan Ya grew up in a divided home. As a young girl she had delayed believing, for the non-Christians had told her she would never get married if she became a Christian. "Look at all those lady missionaries. They haven't found husbands", they said. This was a daunting prospect in a land where everyone gets married. Surely it was right to think about marital prospects first, and then later, perhaps, the question of believing could be dealt with. But the Lord would not allow her to feel content with this decision, and she finally said to the Lord: "If you don't want me to be married, I accept it. But husband or no husband, I must trust you."

It was Dr. Garland Bare who had led her father, Jer Shar, to faith, and sometime later it was to Garland that she went shyly and almost tearfully: "When I told the Lord I was willing to stay unmarried, I really meant it. Now what do I do? I have had three proposals. But before I get married I want to study and prepare myself to serve the Lord." She was an intelligent girl and did well at her studies — but they were to be interrupted. A spot on her leg wasn't healing and finally she asked Dr. Garland to prescribe for it. It was diagnosed as cancer and she was told her leg must be amputated.

Jer Shar shrank from this, naturally enough. In addition to a father's normal reaction he had to face severe pressure from non-Christian relatives, for Hmong believe that to lose a limb in this life means that you are crippled and incomplete in the next life. This is too horrible to contemplate, and Jer Shar suffered under their reproaches. Soo Kan Ya herself found it hard to accept. The Lord gave her peace, but of course this was contested during long days of pain and the slow process of learning to use crutches. She was in the hospital for a long time, and one of the hardest things to bear was that her classmates were graduating without her.

The day came when the doctor said no more could be done for her, and she went home to wait for the end. Just about this time, we sat beside her father in a Thai church service and sang:

"Be still my soul. The Lord is on thy side,
Bear patiently the cross of grief and pain.
Leave to thy God to order and provide.
In every way He faithful will remain.
Be still my soul, thy best, thy heavenly
    friend,
Through thorny ways leads to a joyful end."

Tears were rolling down Jer Shar's face as he sang, and we knew he was thinking of his much-loved daughter. It was indeed a thorny way for them all, but one of the joyful consequences was that as her mother saw the Lord's victory and grace in Soo Kan Ya's life, she too submitted to that grace and believed.

It took Soo Kan Ya a year to die, and the last weeks of her life were increasingly filled with pain. Sometimes she was crotchety and impatient with her family, but even so it was obvious that her rebellion had ceased and God was upholding her. While in a coma she had seen a vision of Heaven, a beautiful place with luxuriant trees and flowers and lawns. She saw the places the Lord was making ready for His people — the Garland Bares' mansion was grand and glorious indeed. She met Hmong Christians who had died, and she saw herself, whole in body and able to run vigorously on two strong legs. Finally she saw a radiance and knew the Lord to whom she had given her life was there. After Soo Kan Ya's death, the Lord tenderly comforted her sorrowing family with each recollection of these glimpses of eternal realities.

Of course mistakes may be made, for the devil is subtle enough to try to mislead Christians. A Karen Christian, rather well off by tribal standards, dreamed that a certain plot of land belonging to a poverty-stricken Christian should be given to him. He went to the Christian headman and told his dream, and the headman was perplexed. It did not seem right to take from a very poor family the bit of land reserved for their son or son-in-law and give it to someone who didn't need it. But if the Lord had spoken, He must be obeyed. The owner of the land was despondent not only at the prospect of losing his land, but that the Lord seemed to be treating him unfairly. It was a delicate situation. After a lot of talking back and forth, the wealthy Karen finally agreed, with reluctance, to set aside his claim. The reluctance was not so much at forfeiting his demand for the land, but at the fact that his dream was regarded as contrary to God's will. Missionaries in such a situation do a great deal of praying for wisdom and for God-honoring solutions to problems that could explode into dissension and trouble.

The devil uses dreams to grip his subjects by fear, to make them powerless to turn to the One who can deal with fear. But the devil doesn't have it all his own way. The Lord uses dreams to warn and to nourish faith. In fact, all the functions of the Word — teaching, rebuking, correcting and training in righteousness — can also be fulfilled in dreams. I firmly believe God ultimately intends to bring His children into the place where they can find His will, His comfort and Himself in the Scriptures. He is likely to wean His children from dependence on dreams and visions. But in the meantime, our work is to use the Word to reinforce truth revealed in vision.

A Christian Akha had been told by the doctor after a long journey to Chiang Mai that nothing could be done for his almost blind eyes. It was a keen disappointment. The missionary prayed for him that night: "Lord, give him good dreams so that he will know you love him and are with him in this trial of his faith." At that time I could not have prayed that prayer, for I did not believe it was valid. But I could pray it today, for I have seen that God does reveal Himself to His needy children in a way that they understand.

Chapter 18

What's Wrong With Poppies?

IF YOU WERE traveling off the beaten track high in the mountains in November, you might stumble on a steep slope of gaily colored poppies, white, fuschia, purple or red, blowing in the breeze. After the corn has been harvested, the same ground is hoed and prepared for the planting of poppy seeds. When the plants are three inches high, several weeks of back-breaking weeding must be done. Then, as the plants flower, the petals fall off and the plant is still green, the pods are scored with a sharp knife. Next morning, before the sun dries it up, the brown substance that oozes through the scratches is collected. That is raw opium from the famed Golden Triangle.

Many tribal folk depend on the sale of opium for their ready cash. Agriculturists are looking for substitute crops, but there is nothing as lucrative as opium, no other crop that yields so much in such a small acreage. You don't even have to market it — eager buyers come to your very door. Traders carrying chickens, fruit and vegetables used to pass through our Lahu village, and we longed to buy their fresh food, but it was no use asking. They wouldn't sell to someone with no opium to exchange. If they had any produce left and we caught them on their way home, they might be persuaded to take some money for their goods, but it was opium they wanted and opium that brought them to the hills.

Although the Bible does not mention opium, the stranglehold of its evil can be clearly seen. Our early missionaries to the tribal people laid down the rule that no one who planted, traded in, or smoked opium could be baptized. Not that people needed missionaries to tell them it was wrong and enslaving — they clearly knew that, but what was the alternative? Even those who longed to be rid of it all needed it for medicine, as well as for the cash it brought. Those already enslaved needed the drug to be able to work. There is nothing in the tribal culture equivalent to the drug scene amongst young people in the Western world. Addiction in nearly all cases starts with ill health and the need for relief from pain. But what begins as a helpful friend ends as an unrelenting enemy. And so the stories of the first Christians in each tribal group are filled with struggle over this issue.

Gung, an attractive twelve-year-old Hmong girl, was in the Barbaras' reading class, and her heart was tender towards the Lord. Her mother had been ill for a long time and finally Gung said to her: "Why don't you believe in Jesus? None of the demon worship has helped you." Her mother assented and that evening Gung was sent over to the missionaries' house with a request for prayer. Next morning the mother was completely better, and seemed convinced by this answer to prayer that it was the Lord who could meet her needs. But Gung's mother and father were on opium. As they lived in just one small room, from her baby days Gung had smelled the sickly sweet fumes from the opium pipes, and when she was sick a bit of opium was given to her. So, very gradually, she too became enslaved, and after her bright beginning she gradually turned away from the Lord. Soon she still had the body of a young girl but the face of a fifty year old, wrinkled and unhealthy. The family haven't strength to do much work but they must earn money for more opium, so in between smoking sessions they work for their neighbors.

This is a terrible captivity, and poses immense problems for the church. It is against Thai law to grow poppies, or to sell or smoke opium, but how can the law be enforced in every tiny, out-of-the-way village in the mountains? In early days police searched some tribal villages, but often the villagers would get wind of the approaching raid. In one village, folk had been burying their opium in the jungle, and early one morning a missionary going out to the forest for a quiet prayer time met an old granny on her way home from hiding her little stock. When she saw him she nodded knowingly, as though she could mention a few hidden spots for his opium cache!

Leona Bair had done a favor for one of her Hmong friends, and was rather taken aback when the friend turned up with a lump of opium as a thank you gift. Finally she said: "I don't think I'd better accept this. You see, it is against the law for me to have it."

"Don't worry, I won't tell anyone," was his cheerful rejoinder. Her gentle insistence that she appreciated his generosity but really *couldn't* accept it finally convinced him that he must allow her to be a law-abiding citizen, and he took the proffered gift home again.

Doong Ye was one of the first Hmong believers, and it was a joy to the missionaries to watch the growth of his enthusiastic faith. As he learned to read he was thrilled with the treasures he found in John's gospel which he took with him to the fields where he spent most of the week. Saturday evenings would find him at the missionaries' house full of questions.

During one of the periods when he was most rejoicing in the Lord, Doe Jones strongly felt she should warn him to be on his guard against small sins that could lead to greater disobedience. The warning was necessary, for he was on opium. His conscience was troubling him, and one morning as the Don Rulison family was praying, Doong Ye stopped by and joined in. He told the Lord that he wanted to give up opium in every way and asked for His help. It was by no means easy. Withdrawal symptoms sent him into complete agony, and at one point he was so ill that Doe feared for his life. She and Mrs. Doong Ye anxiously conferred together. They couldn't sit and watch him die. What should they do? Should they get some opium for him? As they talked, Doong Ye regained consciousness and overheard, and even in his weakness he rebuked them, saying that if

the Lord was willing to suffer for his sin, he must
be willing to suffer to be rid of sin. And he held on
and came through to freedom.

But not for long. He became ill and needed just
a little opium, and immediately he was back in the
old bondage. Several times he tried to break the
habit at a government hospital. At one point he
sold his entire opium stock and his smoking imple-
ments. Then would come more aches and pains,
and with a few puffs to give relief he would be
back at square one. Doong Ye was a leader whose
words carried weight. Even lying on his bed
smoking opium, he would enthusiastically witness
to non-Christians. It was a strange combination,
this man talking about freedom who in some
respects was not free. We who have never known
this terrible craving cannot afford to be censor-
ious, but we cannot help grieving over him.

Prayer for him throughout these years has not
been answered. One night, in a village where he
had gone to buy opium, he heard what he at first
thought was a radio. Over and over again came
the warning about the punishment for those who
trade in opium. He finally went to look for the
radio and could not find it and concluded that it
was God's voice warning him. A day or so later he
was arrested and imprisoned. After his release he
told this experience to a long-standing missionary
friend. "Have you profited by God's warning?"
she asked, knowing he was *not* heeding it. "I've
got to eat," he said carelessly. "God still loves me,
but I've got to eat. You foreigners have pots of

money and you don't know what it is like for us
mountain people." There was a hardness about
him that had not been there earlier. So much
grace, so much blessing prepared for him by the
Lord, and he is missing it all. How will God break
through to people like Doong Ye?

Breaking with opium is traumatic for victim and
missionary alike. To witness the sufferings of
withdrawal, to give such medicines as are possible
for relief, to be on call 24 hours a day for a week at a
time, to be supportive and prayerful, is physically
and emotionally draining. It is worth it all when the
"victim" is freed, but so often he returns to a family
that smokes. Not only must he smell the fumes, but
relatives and friends are quick to offer the pipe,
making resistance as difficult as possible. The
Bevingtons at one time had a room set aside for
people to stay with them and break the habit, with
Rachel's nursing skills close at hand. But even while
staying in the Bevingtons' home, some folk found
friends willing to give them opium secretly, so the
whole purpose was defeated. A Lisu man gave
testimony that God had delivered him even from the
desire to smoke, but six months later he was back on
it again. Even if relatives are supportive, old
illnesses may recur when unchecked by opium.
Father Wood did make the break, but found his
arthritic old body such a burden that he returned to
smoking small amounts. Final relief came for him
only on the day the Lord took him Home.

The Webbs, after many years of experience,
reached the conclusion that there were some people

it was a waste of time and effort to treat: non-Christians who have no spiritual motivation and cannot ask God's help; people who themselves don't really want to break but have been brought by relatives; and people with family members who still plant opium, because the source of supply is too near at hand.

Where, you may ask, is the Lord's power in all this? Is there nothing but failure to report? No, God is still at work and His power is undiminished. Mplia Dua's first attempt at breaking with opium was unsuccessful, but his family stood faithfully with him and encouraged him to try again, and this made all the difference. At his second attempt he realized in a new way that he must draw on the Lord's strength, for his own was not enough. A missionary dreamed that she saw the Lord standing by Mplia Dua's bed, telling him to take His hand and hold on. The dream was an encouragement to Mplia Dua and he did just that — put his own hand in the Lord's firm grasp and was supported through his ordeal. That was many years ago. He and his wife stayed with us once when she was fighting a losing battle with cancer of the jaw, and he was so gentle with her, holding her hand and helping her walk, taking her food that he thought she would like, which is quite un-Hmong-like behavior for a man. Now he himself is old and failing, but these years have been proof of God's power to set free and to maintain that freedom.

Mrs. Ba Ju was the only Christian in her family. Her husband initially said he wanted to be a believer but he soon returned to the old ways and Mrs. Ba Ju had to walk a lonely path. She wanted to be baptized and, rather than face his wrath and his forbidding, went ahead without telling him, feeling that whatever he did he couldn't "unbaptize" her. When he discovered what she had done he was furious and took a knife to her. Fearful for her life she managed to get away, and stayed away until his ire was dampened and it was safe to return.

She too longed to be free of opium. Wanting to truly trust the Lord, and knowing her family would be less than sympathetic, she told no one of her purpose but simply stopped. Perhaps she can be forgiven for feeling a bit smug at this victory. She later told the missionaries how she would lie in bed beside her husband as he smoked — the supreme test is to smell the opium and see others enjoying it — and feel slightly superior to him and to others who were still slaves. Despite this pardonable pride, she did recognize the Victor and she did desperately need Him, for her life was to be a difficult and tragic one. In answer to those lonely prayers for her family, one of her grandsons has been to Bible School, though she never lived to see it. I expect she now knows and rejoices.

Others too have fought this opium battle and won. One Hmong Christian's almost lyrical description of the joys of being opium-free made folk envious of her freedom. A young Akha man who wanted to believe was an addict, and the missionaries wondered about the struggle ahead. But A Shah, one of the Akha Christians, gave them encouragement. He said: "It doesn't matter how much the man has smoked nor how long he smoked. He can break with the Lord's help and the backing of the church here, and no medicine." A Shah could say this with certainty, for he spoke from experience. More and more we have realized that, as one missionary puts it: "The opium battle must be fought on the ground of prayer." To see opium itself as the great enslaver is to miss part of the picture. Behind it is the Evil One who hates to see the Lord setting captives free.

Of recent years the price of opium has become so high that many tribal people, especially those who don't grow it themselves, are going to government centers for help, usually in groups for moral support. Those centers use medicine to help people break off, but I have no idea how many cures are permanent.

The Akha church has taken on the responsibility of helping Akha believers, for they realize that medicine is not sufficient for complete healing. In 1979 YaJu and some of the church elders journeyed to one Akha village where ten new believers wanted to break with opium. The time for this was chosen carefully, in May when the field work was light. "Breaking" is not attempted during field clearing, rice planting or harvest because the work is hard and the smokers would not be strong enough. The medicine used, in decreasing quantities each day, was a mixture of opium, quinine and *baw joe*, an Akha medicine made from insects dried in the sun. All were given vitamin pills and, for those who needed them, sleeping pills. Many of the villagers were involved in the ministry of encouragement and prayer when withdrawal pains were intense. Sometimes the young people's choir was called in to sing to anyone who was in special suffering. During the day the elders visited the homes of the ten "patients", and their teaching from the Word, especially the accounts of Jesus' healings, brought encouragement. They would also pay a last visit at midnight to be sure all the men were at rest and everything was in order. The Lord ministering through the Word, prayer and tender loving care brought these men through to victory.

How I wish I could end on this note. But no. One of the men started to take a little opium in secret. Nothing remains secret for long in a tribal village and one by one, emboldened by the example of the others, all ten went back to their pipes. In prayer the victory can be gained. Without it new believers are likely to sink back further and further into the quicksand. J.O. Fraser, missionary to the Lisu in China, was one who proved the power of continued and united prayer. After just such a time of defeat he wrote: "The powers of darkness need to be fought. I am now setting my face like a flint; if the work seems to fail, then pray; if services fall flat, then pray still more; if months slip by with little or no result, then pray still more and get others to help you."[1]

---

[1] *Mountain Rain* by Eileen Crossman (OMF)

Almost as great a struggle ensues over the issue of planting. (In fact it is slightly ridiculous to talk about planting opium for you actually plant poppy seeds and get opium, but "planting" is the accepted term.) Here too there has been heartbreak, as missionaries have rejoiced over believers' decisions not to plant and have then seen the decisions reversed. The records of the early days read like the ebb and flow of battle. "Despite their decision against opium last year, the Hmong Christians have gone ahead and made opium fields." And, "Everyone is digging ground to plant opium, even some Yao believers who did not plant last year and claimed they would not plant again." But then sounds a word of encouragement. Noah had stopped planting opium, and later, had started again. Doe Jones had no idea of this but felt constrained to speak very forthrightly about disobedience to God's will. It was just the word needed, for Noah felt the sermon to be directly aimed at him and, much to the annoyance of his wife, who at that point did not have such a tender conscience, uprooted his complete poppy crop.

Once on an evangelistic trip Brother Six was asked what he was doing about opium. He was humble about it, saying that no Christian should have any part in it at all, but although he had stopped smoking his faith was not yet strong enough to stop dealing in it. His honest confession made his hearers realize that this was no superhuman, but a Yao man facing the same temptations they were. The day arrived when he and others decided they must obey, and tried planting peppers as a substitute. The pepper crop was eaten by caterpillars. All steps of obedience are contested, but the Lord enabled them to suffer the loss knowing it was better to be out of pocket than in sin.

It seems that these days the tribal churches in general are more tolerant about opium, especially trading in it, than they were a few years ago. The result of compromise is exactly the same in the tribal hills as it is on the streets of San Francisco: it means spiritual loss. This infernal quicksand that sucks in its victims needs to be attacked by prayer in the Lord's name, so that people may see their sin and may be freed.

For many months the North Thailand field were praying for new believers amongst the Pwo Karen who had potential for leadership, that they would take responsibility in their villages and be able to teach simple Bible stories. The leaders were named: some needed to be literate; some needed to be free for teaching. Three needed victory over whiskey; two needed victory over opium. If this surprises and upsets me then I need to remind myself that Western countries have a value system that has been shaped by the Bible. I do not say that we follow our ideals, but we know what the "do's and don'ts" are — or we used to. The flagrant sins of the flesh are condemned in our Christian circles, and rightly so. It is devastating to a new missionary to find that new believers regard premarital sex as an accepted and natural custom. It seems obvious to us that this matter, and such things as opium addiction, should be dealt with immediately. But this is by no means obvious to the new convert. He is aware of his need to be delivered from demonic power. He is taking his first stumbling steps in a world where he can now disregard the demons and taboos, and he is unsettled, insecure. He does not yet see his ethical problems. God does, and He is going to lead His children in a growing relationship with Himself, He who is a holy God and who has made provision for our holiness.

We tend to weigh sins on a scale, thinking the heaviest are the sins of the flesh, and the lighter are the sins of the spirit — pride, jealousy and indifference to the needs of others. But this is not biblical. Surely God hates my bad temper as much as, or more than, He hates the opium addiction of a Karen.

I am not saying temperance and chastity are unimportant, but that drunkenness, immorality, touchiness and vanity all keep us from enjoying the Lord's presence. They equally hide His light, the light that should reach others. My sin may have little effect on others or it may be devastating to my neighbor, but it is still sin, to be abhorred and forsaken. God is going to deal with all these things as we yield Him His rights as Lord. If I who have been a Christian for some forty years still have battles over pride and irritability, I should be able to pray with sympathy and understanding for my Akha and Karen brothers who fight their battles with liquor and opium. We have the privilege of committing ourselves, and them, into the hands of the One who, as the writer of Acts put it "sent His Son to bless us in turning us away from our sins."

Chapter 19

To Suffer For His Sake

MISSIONARIES KNOW THAT to share God's good news with a tribal person *may* make him a candidate for grace — it will certainly make him a candidate for trouble. From the moment he shows any interest in the Gospel he is, in a sense, a marked man. Our "ancient foe" notes the interest and sets out to dampen the enthusiasm before it issues in decision and commitment. Even if he fails in this attempt, he doesn't stop. He can make life very uncomfortable for a new believer.

When Ted and Nell Hope first met Wu Di he had already performed all the usual spirit ceremonies that a Lisu does in time of illness, and he was still ill. The Gospel the Hopes shared with him was attractive, and even more inviting was Ted's offer to take him for medical help in Chiang Mai. But the doctors there said that nothing could be done for him, and when Wu Di heard this verdict he turned away from the Lord's offer of grace and seemed callous and hard. However, in answer to prayer his attitude changed, and his very helplessness was a constant reminder to him that help, of a spiritual nature, was available.

When Wu Di first told his wife of his interest in being a Christian, she said bluntly that if he believed she would leave him and take their only child with her. The headman showed how he felt about the idea when he announced that Wu Di would be made to pay a fine if he should persist in this foolishness. Deterred by these threats Wu Di made no outward move, but he still longed for the Lord's comfort.

His second attempt to convince the family of the benefit of walking the Lord's way only brought the response that he would have to walk it alone. If he believed, he must fend for himself. He was too ill to work, had no money and was dependent on his relatives for food and clothing. To become a Christian was to put himself beyond his family's duty to help him. He knew the neighbors would not dare to interfere. What should he do? He could not live without food.

For a time he refused to take part in the demon worship, but he was unable to muster enough courage for an open confession of Christ. Then at the last, in increasing weakness and pain, seeing no way out and unconvinced that the God he had never seen could do for him what his family would not do, he gave up the struggle and asked for the old familiar demon ceremonies. He died soon after.

We can hardly blame relatives who feel threatened at the thought of one of their family turning to a "foreign religion." Who knows what calamity will fall upon the family of anyone who deserts the path of the spirits? If their hearts are not open to the truth, if they are not attracted to this new way of life, they can't understand the inquirer's longings, only try to convince him of his madness.

But what if he persists and believes? There are still ways and means of turning him from his delusions. As long as old Father Wood lived, the family were grudgingly allowed to call themselves Christians. But after he died, Mother Wood went to her fields one morning to find some neighbors working there. They told her, "The headman says you have chosen to turn away from our clan laws, so you have no claim to any land here." Mother Wood had to have fields for rice growing, so she turned back to the demon ways as the headman intended. Even if a missionary had been there, it would have been useless to appeal to the headman, for this would only have called down more wrath upon the family. As far as we know, Mother Wood has never felt free to walk openly in faith.

There is no way missionaries can shield people from the opposition of family and neighbors. In a land where for centuries Satan has had things his own way, there is no escape from ostracism and trouble for a new believer. Sometimes it is just teasing. When a Christian Lawa boy said grace before his meals in the school lunch hour he had to endure many mocking remarks. "Umpone has to have a little nap before he eats," they would joke. None of us, especially teenagers, enjoy being laughed at.

Sometimes there is skillful persuasion to turn back. Sometimes threats are used. Drew's Hmong relatives threatened to drive him away if he didn't return to the demon way, but he stood firm, saying he couldn't change. He knew the only true God, the God who loved him, and how could he turn away from One like that? Perhaps his very boldness daunted them, for they didn't follow through on their threats. More often these are carried out. The lad At was forbidden by his parents to take part in Christmas worship and festivities; he was beaten and forced to take part in the family spirit ceremonies instead. For the missionaries to interfere would have made it harder for him, but they prayed and stood with him, and gave him love. But the beating hurt, as did the anger of At's parents at what seemed to them incredible disloyalty.

Old Grandfather Chieh Shua had been bed-ridden for years and when he and his family believed the Christians prayed for his healing. But this was not granted, and finally his sons said that if Jesus wasn't going to heal him they must revert to the old demon ways. His wife did not agree with this decision, but the sons went ahead with the spirit ceremonies. When there was still no change in his condition, they told their mother it was her fault the demons weren't answering; she too must turn back to the demons. In her perplexity Mrs. Chieh Shua came to consult Doe Jones.

"Would it be all right", she asked, "to tell the family that I will serve the spirits again? It would just be a matter of words, for in my heart I'm fully convinced Jesus is Lord and intend to serve Him. It's only for my husband's sake..."

Doe longed to shield her from suffering but knew there was only one possible answer to such a question.

As the husband was ill his right to whip a disobedient wife was given to his sons, and they beat her severely. That day she entered into the "fellowship of His suffering", and she did not turn back. New reserves of grace came to her. Now she knew that God could be counted on even in suffering, and longed that others should share her joy. When she discovered a young foreign couple — tourists who had found their way to the village — were not Christians, she pled with them to believe. Doe had to translate her words, of course, but no translation was needed for her face, which shone with loving concern for them. The Hmong church hold her in high esteem, for through the years she has been a guardian of truth and uprightness. She has no time for compromise, nor patience with compromisers. Truth to tell, she is dictatorial and difficult to live with, for she feels it her duty to point out the failures and sins of her large family. But I expect the day will come when they too will realize that she has scolded them because she cares about them and wants them to wholly follow the Lord.

There are other ways of expressing family disapproval. A Lu had destroyed his demon shelf with its bowls and streamers and incense, and had turned to the Lord with all his family. Soon after this, they were forced to give up their eldest son to the clan of the wife's late husband, for the clan said the ancestors had been sinned against when the family became Christians. Resistance against the power of the clan would have been useless, and the grieving parents had to hand him over. A little Yao widow had a similar sorrow. Her twelve-year-old son was taken from her because the husband's family had no intention of letting him believe too. To surrender your child to unbelieving relatives can bring nothing but pain.

When a Karen is ill a feast is held for the spirits, in which every member of the family must take part. The elderly mother of one of the Christians was sick, and the family were anxious about her, wanting to do everything they could to bring help and healing. So they prepared a spirit feast. The Christian may be prepared to trust God for his own health, but can he trust for his unbelieving mother? If he refuses to eat, what should he say to his family when they accuse him of being unwilling to help his mother, or blame him for her continuing illness? At least one of the church leaders felt unable to face his family's outrage and partook of this ceremonial meal. No doubt it seemed to him a small but inevitable compromise; but it is a dangerous one. However, we who have never faced such a choice cannot afford to be critical. It would be more appropriate if we were moved to prayer.

Because he had become a Christian, Mr. Poot's neighbors refused to lend him their buffalo to plow his rice fields before planting. This was a terrible blow to him. His first idea was that the missionaries should buy a buffalo for him and he would pay them back later. Instead they prayed together about the need, and another neighbor agreed to lend his buffalo. Mr. Poot was delighted at this answer, for he was only just beginning to learn of the Lord's ability to meet His children's practical needs. Had the missionaries complied with his request — and it would have been easy to do such a humanitarian thing — he would have learned to trust the missionary instead.

In a Yao village where a number of folk had believed, the pressure from those in official positions was severe. One woman said that they were now regarded as "outsiders" by their neighbors. This sense of not belonging is impossible to bear unless there is a greater sense of belonging to the Lord. The pressure for conformity is specially heavy for anyone in authority, like Mooling, who is a headman and responsible for the welfare of the folk in his small town. They demand his participation in the demon rites that concern everybody, and it takes a very firm faith and solid commitment to face losing your position, as Mooling would certainly do if he refused. So far he has felt unable to refuse for this reason, and so he compromises, avoiding the conflict but with spiritual loss.

When our Marilyn was just a youngster she was facing some difficult problem, and I was in a lather about it, praying that the Lord would spare her. At last the Lord seemed to say to me, "Are you going to shield this child from all opportunities for growth? Are you going to shelter her so she will never learn to trust me?" I was shocked to realize my mother instinct was doing exactly that — robbing my child of lessons in faith. The missionary feels this same protective longing for the babes in Christ. We find ourselves wishing we could save them from stress and strain, longing to whisk them away from the stifling social pressure and the suffering of loneliness. We have to learn there is no way we can save them from ostracism, or restore their lost place in the clan structure. Standing alongside, suffering with them, praying for them, sharing our certainty of God's sovereign control is one path open to us, and it is open even to those who cannot be physically present.

"Remember those who are in prison as though you were in prison with them. Remember those who are suffering as though you were suffering as they are," is a command from Scripture that applies here. Even from a distance we can remember those who suffer, feel with them and let pity and concern move us to pray that they will be reminded that God has not deserted them. We can pray that regardless of their feelings, they will hold to the *fact* of His presence; that they will prove, even as we have, that He is an ever-present help in trouble.

Chapter 20

Treasure Chest

THERE IS A treasure chest in the Chiang Mai Mission Home. It is a large cupboard made of teak, filled with gaily-covered books and booklets. You would not find them interesting reading, but to those of us who have spent months of arduous work on producing those materials, they are treasure indeed. Some missionary has had to learn the language from scratch, reduce it to writing, compile and print dictionaries, primers, readers, gospels and hymnbooks. That one sentence of 23 words takes only a moment to read, but it spans years of strenuous labor.

No missionary can do this alone and informants were hard to find. They were busy in their fields and tired when they came home at night, and they also had to get used to the idea of books. The ideal Hmong, for example, rises early and works hard all day. He does not sit lazily with a book in front of him. Nor could the people at first see much importance in this matter that the missionary put so much stress on. But gradually the Christians began to understand what the Word did for the missionaries, and the day came when Noah said, "When problems come up, the missionaries find the answers from portions of the Word that we do not have in Hmong." That's when he saw that translation was a priority, not a lazy waste of time, and Noah was a great help in the early translation days. Others may have been keener intellectually, but they gave less consistent help than Noah with his insight and motivation.

Nowadays there are tribal Christians who can read Thai, and so the Thai Scriptures can be the basis for translation. In our early days this was not the case, so the translation helpers were dependent on the missionary to give them the content of the Word. Eric Cox, working with three Yao Christians, would tell them the meaning of a passage. Each would write out his draft of that verse, then Eric would type them up, after noting any omissions or misunderstandings. When several passages had been done in this way, the drafts would be compiled into a joint rendering, which was mimeographed and put into test use in the church. Church members' opinions were channeled back to the committee so that necessary changes could be made.

Inevitably, all the translating groups had cultural problems to solve. Paul's journeys by ship, for example, were a mystery to people who had never seen either an ocean or a large boat. Words to describe spiritual truths such as atonement and resurrection, and even a word for God, took some hunting for.

Translation is a battle, something Satan is contesting along every line. One of his weapons was sickness, which plagued the translators' teams with one thing after another: a bad eye infection, cholera, flu, sprue. Brother Six, whose stability and knowledge of his own Yao language was such an encouragement, was often ill and finally became so frail that he could no longer participate. The work had to slow down when field work became heavy, and then it was hard to get everyone moving again. It was desperately difficult to be patient over what seemed unreasonable delays. How the Yao team rejoiced when finally, on the last day of 1972, the first translation of the New Testament from Mark to Revelation was completed.

This whole translation program included many long hours at the typewriter. One Hmong missionary reckoned that, if everything went well, it would take from February through July to type the White Hmong New Testament. An informant who had begun work on Mark's Gospel by himself gave his first chapters to Doris Whitelock to type, adding that he was tired of writing o's so from henceforth he would not bother with them. This did not make for easy deciphering of his manuscript! As Doris put it, "Hw wuld yu enjy a bk t read withut any o's?"

Of course, it is no use having Bibles if no one can read them. So there must be a literacy program, which means books to learn to read from, and people to make them, helped by the artistic members of the team. In the early days in China there was no typewriter for the Hmong script and one missionary wrote out the entire New Testament three times by hand! But now we have typewriters and scanners and mimeograph machines.

I confess I have not always been thankful for the latter two aids, however. I am an awkward, heavy-handed creature and machines, like dogs, know I am afraid of them and act accordingly. During my many hours of cranking a duplicator I learned they are inexplicable animals. The paper could be running through beautifully and then, for no reason at all, everything would go haywire. After much fussing and fuming on my part, and dutifully checking of such mechanics as I was capable of, I would have to drag my husband out of his study. He would look over the situation, try the machine and find it was working beautifully! I did learn a few mechanical tricks and after months of using the machines I became a little more confident. In one of my confident periods a friend wanted to know who paid for my mistakes. "Oh," I airily replied, "I don't make many mistakes these days." And turning back to my task, I blithely printed a hundred pages upside down. There are 97 gray hairs on my head put there by my mimeographing efforts. Heaven will, I expect, be engine free; or if it isn't then the engines will work and I will know how to handle them.

It is not difficult to persuade tribal youngsters to come to reading classes, even if these are held at 6 a.m. before work begins in the fields. Adults are usually slower to learn a new skill so foreign to their culture, and are apt to lose heart. And there are definite hindrances. Ruth Wyss wrote about a demon priest, "He is trying hard to stop the literacy classes and has already succeeded in keeping most of the men away from them. The devil truly seems to be afraid of literate Akha."

Just when the time came that we could rejoice over the good stocks in that teak cupboard, we heard of a new government ruling. "No romanized script can be used in tribal language printing. All literature must be produced in Thai script." Overnight, almost all the books in our cupboard had become obsolete. Hundreds of Akha New Testaments had just been reprinted, and a new literacy course compiled. Not only would the hymnbooks and the Scriptures have to be retyped, but the literacy courses and the primers were now useless.

By God's grace the job was tackled. The Akha team had been increasingly aware of the differences between the Thailand and Burma dialects. The New Testament they were using had been translated in Burma, and since it must now be reprinted anyway they decided to do a new translation which would be more readable for Thailand Akha.

Only the Pwo Karen, who were already using Thai script, were unaffected by this ruling. For the tribal Christians who must now learn to read the Thai script, which is more difficult than romanized, the end is not yet in sight. I am afraid that the old grannies who found learning romanized such a trauma will not have the courage to start again.

In the early days of the Hmong work, Mrs. Jia Dza was struggling with the printed pages of the small primer. Suddenly she looked up with wonder on her face, and said, "When I finish this primer, then I can read the Scriptures!" It was worth all the labor to hear that one remark. All who have been involved in the translating and printing of the Word are richly rewarded as we hear how God is using it to shape lives. One of my most valued pictures is of a Pwo Karen Christian wedding. The groom and his bashful little bride, with her face turned away, are sitting on the floor, and as they make their vows they are laying their hands on a Scripture portion. I printed that Scripture. I have a part in the spiritual growth of young Karen people.

Gau is a refugee, and poor. Neighbors let their buffalo into his corn patch so often and he knew it was deliberate. He could not afford the loss of his crop, and so he put poison on the grass and leaves surrounding the edges of his fields. That should put an effective end to the trespassers! And then he was faced by the Word that says we are to do good to them that hate us, and to love our enemies. He realized that he had sinned and confessed this before the Lord — but how do you un-poison a field? The Lord accomplished it for him by sending heavy rains that effectively washed the poison off the plants! And Gau prayed for grace to truly love the people who were trying to harm him.

Forest is skillful at playing the Hmong pipes, and was much in demand at funerals when the pipes are used to escort the dead person's spirit into the after life. For a time after he became a Christian he continued to do this, feeling it was a good opportunity to be helpful. Then he began to feel uneasy about a practice that he knew to be false, but found it very difficult to say "No", especially to members of his own clan. He was truly disturbed by the verse that said: "If we go on sinning willfully after receiving the knowledge of the truth, there no longer remains a sacrifice for sin." Finally he wrote to Jonah, one of the leading Christians, and asked him what he should do. Jonah answered with the Word from Galatians in the Hmong version: "In the past you did not know God, and so you were slaves of beings who are not gods. But now that you know God, how is it that you want to turn back to those weak and pitiful ruling spirits?" That clinched the matter. Refusal to play the pipes was hard, but it issued in new spiritual power in Forest's life.

The Word brought the Lord's comfort to him too. Forest's father-in-law had been really cantankerous, refusing to pay any damages although his cattle got into Forest's fields. He also took some of his daughter Va's dowry, including embroidery that her now-dead mother had earmarked for her, and gave it to someone else. This was more than a financial loss; it was intended to hurt Va, and it did. It was hard not to feel bitter, and they questioned the missionary whether the Word had anything to say about this. Of course it did and the Lord ministered to them, bringing healing to their hurt.

Bun Yay had believed as a young boy while staying in a Christian hostel. He didn't know much of the Word but he had taken for his own the verse, "With God all things are possible." One day he was out in the fields with his mother and some younger brothers and sisters, when his sister's nose started to bleed. This is a bad omen to the Hmong, and demon worship should be done. But nothing helped and finally his mother said to him: "You are a Christian, you pray." His mind filled with fear. How could he, an eleven-year-old boy, pray for such a thing? But remembering that all things are possible, he reminded the Lord of this promise and asked for healing. The bleeding stopped instantly.

Mark had to make a choice. He wanted to move back to his home village to be near his parents, where he could also help in the church. He longed for the security of the familiar spot and dreaded moving to an area where there were no believers. But he was even more concerned about what God wanted. Being distrustful of people who said they had great flashes from heaven to guide them, for most of a week he set aside time for prayer, fasting and reading the Word. On the final day he read Isaiah 49:6, which in the Hmong rendering says: "The Lord said, I have a greater task for you, my servant. I will make you a light so that others may be saved." He knew that the servant directly addressed was Christ, but he was sure God was telling him that to settle at home was the easy thing. The greater task was to reach out to other

Hmong and allow them to enjoy the Light. So the decision was made. He moved to an area where there were no Christians and God's light shone in their lives. He has moved several times since then, and at each move there has been a fresh fulfilling of that promise.

Doris Whitelock, plodding along with Corinthians in her translation of the White Hmong Scriptures in Laos, asked the Lord for some encouragement. How good it would be to know that the Word was having its effect in people's lives! Soon after this, a Hmong woman came in from the mountains and said: "I don't know what is the matter with my eighteen-year-old daughter Lou. She only went to Lao school for one year and refused to go back again. She wasn't at all interested in books. But this past year, since the Hmong books have come, I can't get her to stop reading them. She reads the Scripture till all hours of the night and I tell her she'll never be able to get up in the morning to go to the fields, but she just goes on reading. The tears stream down her face as she thinks about her sin, and she wants so much to do God's will. I gave her money to buy a new blouse, and she went off and bought more Scripture portions." What more could a missionary ask for?

Some years later Lou left Laos as a refugee and spent four years in the camp where Doris was then working. She was depressed at times, for the other members of the family had already gone to the States, but always her heart was tender towards the Lord. Her babies were sickly and she and Doris often prayed together for them. One day as they prayed she thanked the Lord for His goodness and His provision. She was a refugee. Her house, inside the confining fence of the camp, was a miserable place with cardboard walls. Her baby was crying and fretful. But Lou had eyes to see beyond the immediate surroundings. She and her husband and children finally went to the States to join the rest of her family. There, early one morning, someone forced an entry into the house, raped her mother and shot and killed her father. For this to happen in California, the longed-for place of refuge, was particularly bitter. Life will probably never be easy for her, for she is quite deaf and speaks indistinctly, and may never master English. But the Lord of the Book who sustained her in times past will continue to be to her all she needs.

Literacy progress is still our priority prayer. When the romanized script was still acceptable some of the tribal believers were semi-literate. That meant that reading was hard work. If you have ever studied a foreign language and tried to read your Bible in it you will realize something of the difficulty. You are so taken up with figuring out individual words that you don't take in the total meaning. Reading the Word is an exercise in deciphering, and folk often feel too tired in the evenings to tackle it. After four days of concentrated study of the Word one believer sighed and said wearily: "I'm so exhausted even my blood vessels are tired!"

Not many even of those who can read have a daily early morning quiet time in the way we Westerners feel necessary. Partly this is a cultural thing for they are expected to be bright and cheery and at work by the crack of dawn. A Yao widow was finding the Word to be her sustenance and wanted to read it first thing, but the other Christians severely criticized her for her laziness.

It is partly also, however, a lack of spiritual hunger. A Spanish nun once said: "You Protestants have meat but no hunger; here we have much hunger but no meat." Some groups have little appetite, and this is something only prayer can cure, but it is not the total picture. The two Barbaras told how when the Blue Hmong were receiving their New Testaments, two believers stood up one Easter Sunday and gave testimony of verses that were meaningful to them. Some from another group sat up nearly all night reading their new copies, and at dawn went to bed rejoicing. Some do read the Word — like Noah commenting halfway through the day: "I'll have to go and have my quiet time. I can't work without it." It is probably a Western idea that you must have a set time for devotions, but it is true too that having no set time for the Word often means it gets crowded out of the day.

Celia is the living example that poor reading ability does not necessarily discourage from studying the Word. When Oldest Son first showed interest in her, her family let it be know that she could not marry into a Christian family. So his

Hmong Christian family obligingly became "non-Christian" for a time, and Celia's family felt it would now be safe and allowed her to marry Oldest Son. They did not reckon with the fact that Celia would continually be going to the fields with two enthusiastic Christian women. About a year later Celia herself believed, started to learn to read, and prayed continuously for her husband to follow her example. She had read Peter's word about nagging so she relinquished this wifely prerogative, but prayed the more earnestly. Oldest Son's baptism after two years of her praying was a joyful time, and he himself testified that it was his wife's example that made him face his need.

There were testings along the way, of course. A much loved baby died, but the Lord of the Word comforted her. Some years later, Celia became certain of something she had suspected for a long time — her husband was unfaithful to her. She grieved and prayed and waited, but there was no hoped-for miracle. One evening Oldest Son and the girl he had taken for a second wife arrived at the door, called out for her to open it, and casually moved in. This is quite a common occurrence among the Hmong, and has to be accepted by the first wife with as much patience as possible. But Oldest Son was a Christian, though the second wife is not, and he and Celia had had a caring relationship. Who could blame her if she felt bitter?

Leona Bair, a close personal friend of both of them, hurriedly made a trip to their village to comfort Celia, and was herself comforted. It was Celia who encouraged Leona to trust God through this, saying God had given her peace and was filling her heart. As they read Scripture to each other she told how God speaks continually and relevantly in His Word. "I thought I could never cook for her (the second wife) but I remembered 'love your enemies', and because of these words I overcame, and I cook and call her to eat."

During the year when Oldest Son was living elsewhere, Celia established her own nightly routine, after the children were in bed. She would read aloud five pages of the Bible, sing ten hymns and pray out loud. She reads *painfully* slowly, but her heart seeks the living God so she finds Him. Or rather He finds her. It doesn't matter that she is semi-literate. Earlier she had said to Leona: "I want the Word to rule my life," and this was a sincere desire, but it cannot be maintained automatically and sometimes she has forgotten her purpose. Perhaps she was buoyed up by the hope that God would soon answer her prayers.

Faith burned brightly at first, for God had so wonderfully met with her. But some years have elapsed with no change in her situation. Oldest Son has been disciplined by the elders, and he is bitter. He says he still believes in his heart but will never return to the church. There is no sign of any relief, and there must be days when Celia questions the love and goodness of God. When the new wife had her babies and was free from field work for a month, Celia was unhappy about doing the extra work and let her dissatisfaction be known. Because Oldest Son is headman of the village it is his wife's duty to feed any guests. The villagers say Celia has not done her duty, so he may well feel he has the right to the help of the new wife. The trial of Celia's faith continues as she lives daily with the other woman and her children.

A severe trial can be faced with poise if we know it will soon be over. The assurance of coming relief makes bearable the present distress. A friend used to say she wanted to learn patience and she wanted to learn it in a hurry! But neither patience nor longsuffering can be learned in a hurry, and they are often learned when God *seems* to be absent. This makes great demands on us, "having little connection with feeling, and not achieved without deliberate continuous costly effort of heart, mind and will."[1] Is this the present lesson set for Celia to learn? We know that God is the Lord of the Word, the One who first held her to her duty and comforted the lonely places in her heart. In answer to prayer, He will continue to be to her all that she needs.

In the lessons that the Lord sets us to learn, His textbook is His Word. Of course the enemy makes a determined effort to keep us from this textbook. A busy life full of interruptions, the heat, and a perpetual sense of tiredness all play their part. When Dr. Cochrane of the Leprosy Mission had had a very strenuous schedule in Thailand, some-

---

[1] *Fruits of the Spirit* by Evelyn Underhill

one asked if he was tired. "The word 'tired' is not in my vocabulary," was his firm answer. I admire that spirit, but I can't emulate it. The word "tired" *is* in my vocabulary, so I need to pray for a disciplined spirit.

Missionaries, like other people, must carefully guard their time with the Lord. We have all the familiar problems. Wandering thoughts, for example. I pick up my Bible in the morning and have an overwhelming urge to write out my marketing list, or make sure I put addresses on the letters I wrote the night before! Mothers with small children have to fight for time for devotions. One missionary mother said she had been jumping up and down all through the mealtime to attend to other people's needs, and she herself got fed in small installments. Afterwards the Lord showed her, "Today you did not have an uninterrupted time to eat, but you were fed. You can get enough food in small bites. If you will allow me to, I can give you your spiritual food in that way, so don't fret about not having large portions of time." If we have an appetite, God will see to it that we have food for our souls.

Sometimes as children in school we sat half-heartedly listening, with no intent to remember what was being taught. We can read God's Word that way. Through force of habit or because we know we ought to we open the sacred pages, but with little intent to remember what we read or to be changed by it. It is not that we deliberately turn away from the truth — it is more insidious and therefore more deadly than that. It is possible to be a missionary lacking the eager heart of a learner, as our enthusiasm is almost imperceptibly lost. As C.S. Lewis says: "The safest road to hell is the gradual one — the gentle slope, soft underfoot, without milestones, without signposts."[2] Our attention is gradually given to so many worthy things, that we do not realize we have turned away from our Teacher. Because He is a patient God and He loves us, He will find ways of getting our attention again. The Holy Spirit's work is to convict us of being inattentive pupils. He will not spare us in ensuring that we become the most enthusiastic, the most faithful scholars it is in our power to become.

There are some 560 versions of the Bible in English! In the United States more money is spent on new versions in English than on Bible translation for all the rest of the world. Something is wrong here. I walk through Bible bookstores at home and gaze at the shelves of Bibles, the rows of study helps, the commentaries and the books that have molded my life and given such joy and blessing. I cannot help but compare it with the meager contents of our small teak cupboard at the head of the Mission Home stairs.

And I cannot help but long for Christians who will shoulder the burden of prayer for all that is entailed in refilling and overflowing that teak cupboard — the days of hard study, the crick-in-

---

[2]*Screwtape Letters*

the-neck typing, the laborious correcting of mistakes when everything seems to go wrong, the tedious mimeographing, the days of sometimes discouraging literacy teaching. All who earnestly pray for these things will share in the joy of tribal believers who become people of the Word.

Chapter 21

In God's School of Theology

A CHRISTIAN MAN was knocked down by a car, and after he was hospitalized one friend said to him: "The devil has done this to keep you from the Lord's work." Another said: "God has put you here to be quiet and rest in Him." And his wife said: "Why didn't you look where you were going?" I suspect that temperament will, at least in part, dictate your opinion as to which of these three was correct. They combine to make up the truth.

Untoward circumstances that are not our fault are usually attributed to Satan or to God. The Scriptures force me to believe that even Satan's attacks are used by the Lord to fulfill what He has purposed. Joseph's brothers were not thinking of doing God's will when they put him squarely in the place of God's blessing. The Lord Jesus was, by God's set purpose and foreknowledge, given into the hands of evil men who did with Him what their evil hearts prompted them to do. God raised Him from the death they planned, for He planned our salvation. We are related to our sovereign Lord. We need not fuss too much over the mysterious relation of man's free will and God's foreordination, and may rejoice even when we do not understand.

One of our missionaries said, some years ago when we were discussing problems in the lives of new Karen believers, "They have a faulty concept of God." I didn't reply but inwardly I thought: "How like a man to give an abstruse, theological answer. Lofty concepts are not what they need at this point." But I was wrong. Theology, the study of God, was exactly what they needed. How can they be properly related to Him unless they know who and what He is? Looking back over my forty years as a Christian, I can see that my own gravest problems have arisen because of a mistaken view of God.

All missionary candidates are examined on their theological beliefs, but I found there could be a gap between what I wrote (after much laborious study) on my doctrinal statement, and the truth that I daily enjoyed. I look at my life and the lives of my fellow workers, and I see that God is constantly at work helping us to close that gap. He wants our head knowledge to become heart knowledge, and tests our faith so we may be encouraged to trust Him more boldly. A pastor once pointed out that the trial of our faith is not to find out how faulty it is but to prove how trustworthy He is. I had always pictured God testing me to show how little I believed, but He has a more positive purpose — to increase my capacity to enjoy His faithfulness. Many of the experiences He gives us on the mission field are really lessons in the school of theology. I can present no theological treatise but I can testify that I have gone through trial triumphantly, or in miserable failure, depending upon my hold of the sovereignty of God.

His lessons concerning His sovereignty often center around great distress. It was so in the story of Jia Dunn, a Hmong headman who had shown interest in the Gospel for a year or so before he believed. He delayed because he felt he must first perform the ceremony for releasing the spirits of his parents, but when he did believe he proved to have spiritual insight. He early learned about the holiness of God and when he was a six-month-old Christian he prayed: "Lord, help me to distinguish clearly between right and wrong. Give me a bold heart that I may not be afraid to say what is right." This was a courageous prayer for a headman, for the quickest route to unpopularity is to stand against sin.

People often came seeking his advice while he was in church, and the Hmong way would have been to attend to them immediately. But he courteously requested that they wait till the worship service was over. He was wise in counseling and at one of the first Hmong conferences he and others did much to encourage those from other villages in the faith. What to do if there are bad omens like a snake coming in the house or a bird flying in? Can we do magic to cure sickness? Jia Dunn and other older Christians dealt with each of these puzzling matters, assuring the believers that Jesus was a safe retreat in every trial, a faithful listener to our prayers, and a sufficient Savior for now and eternity. It was obvious that here was one of God's "choice ones", one who could help others.

During this time, however, he was still trading in opium. But the Lord brought him to the point of being ready to make a complete break with it, and one day he gathered up his opium store and traveled down to the plain to sell it all, after which he planned to be baptized. It had been a long tiring journey; Jia Dunn and his companions were glad to retire for the night. Then suddenly he sat up, gasped once, and was dead. It was unbelievable! A spate of wild rumors began about what Jesus and the foreigners had done to him. His own family immediately returned to the spirits, and a gun was fired three times to get rid of God the Father, God the Son and God the Holy Spirit. Not only was it a blow to the small struggling Hmong church, who missed Jia Dunn at every turn, but the missionaries could not help wondering why. He was so promising. His position as headman had shown the Hmong that a man of influence could be a Christian. His heart was set on doing God's will. *Why*, then? We do not know. The Sovereign God gave no answers to His wondering servants. They only knew that a loving Heavenly Father had taken one of His children Home.

This lesson has been set to us as a field a number of times, for the mastery of one lesson does not automatically ensure the mastery of the next. Some years later a group of our North Thailand missionaries were gathered one evening for fellowship, prayer and music. We had had a prayer meeting and were getting ready to practice the choir numbers we were to sing at conference, when the Mission Home dog set up a commotion at the arrival of the telegraph boy with two telegrams. We laughed heartily over the mistakes on the addresses of the wires, and then Larry opened them. The contents simply could not be true. Missionary Peter Wyss and his friend Sammy Schweitzer, who was on a brief visit from Switzerland, had been robbed and killed. We were totally stunned.

Peter and Sammy had traveled to an Akha village, going as far as they could by motor bike and walking the remaining distance. There they stayed the night. Next morning Peter's wife Ruth and a fellow missionary went out to the village where the bike had been left to await the men's return. When they didn't come the ladies returned to the Wyss home, thinking perhaps Peter and Sammy were hurrying to catch Sammy's midday plane and had come out by a different route. But when there was still no sign of them, Ruth set out with two missionary friends towards the Akha village. Along the trail they found the bodies of the two men.

All of the North Thailand missionary family gathered in Chiang Rai for the funeral service. As the choir sang, "Unto the hills around do I lift up my longing eyes," I believed every word and yet my heart was protesting and questioning. For what does the Psalm say? "My help comes from the Lord who made heaven and earth." Lord, when the robbers sprang out from the sheltering trees, were you suddenly absent from that corner of your created world? "He who keeps you will not slumber. The Lord will protect you from all evil." A broken arm, a stab wound, bullets. Were these not evil? "The Lord will guard your going out and your coming in." Your two servants went out to do your will in your service, but they did not come in.

Peter had been our superintendent. We had profited by his leadership and his example. He was so needed by his wife and three children, and by the North Thailand missionary family. Again, the Lord gave us no explanation. We know that He need never account to us for what He does, but we still long to know there is meaning in the events He brings. He is not an impersonal God, not capricious, not bound by the world and people He created. The men who took Peter's life did not slip in and attack when God's attention was diverted. When we returned to our conference after the funeral, one of the speakers asked us, "What would you think of the captain of an army who said to his men, 'You are going into battle. All of you will return unharmed'?" No captain would promise this, nor does our Heavenly Captain promise warfare without wounds or casualties. The word "casualty" suggests a chance affair, someone just "happening" along at the wrong moment. Peter and Sammy were not casualties in that sense. It was their Father's work that took them into that ambush. He said their work was accomplished, their warfare done, and quickly they were in His immediate presence.

This much we knew. We were set the lesson of trusting Him, our questions unanswered.

Not all God's lessons center in tragedy. Learning to submit to God often involves submitting to fellow missionaries. There are times when we would like to change this, for it is one thing to accept what a loving God ordains and quite another to accept what a fellow missionary plans for us. We have an elected field council that advises the superintendent about concerns such as the placing of workers. The members of this group are just human beings like the rest of us. They are as liable to be swayed by their own temperaments as we are; their home background and secular training influence the way they see things; they have quirks and pet theories, just like the rest of the human race; they may even have a few prejudices. And they are the ones who make decisions for us. What is the link, then, between their fallible judgments and the sovereignty of God? It is at this point that we can get into trouble. We know the field council are concerned for the glory of God and for the work of His church, and that they have prayed over their decision. But even so we sometimes question those decisions.

It is humanly impossible to see the needs of the neighboring tribe as clearly as your own. If the Akha and the Yao teams get the only two new missionaries, the Hmong and the Karen teams must come to terms with the fact that, seemingly, someone else's needs are being met and theirs are not. Did the council *really* choose rightly? We may be tempted to blame them for our lack of helpers, but this is fatal. If we see ourselves in the hands of men we can expect to be miserable, but if we know ourselves to be in God's hands, subject to His decisions, we can go on in peace. Amy Carmichael speaks of learning to welcome God's will even when it comes via the plans of others. She says, "Stormy wind fulfilling His word — by the time the wind blows upon us it is His wind for us. We have nothing to do with what first of all stirred up that wind. It could not ruffle a leaf on the smallest tree in the forest had He not opened the way for it to blow through the fields of air. He commandeth even the winds and they obey Him."[1]

Oswald Sanders once said that the supreme test of our spirituality is our reaction to life's inequalities. We get concerned when other people appear to have more privileges than we have, or easier living conditions, or fewer problems. We may be too proud to express these concerns publicly, but we still have private comparison sessions where we note our lacks, as opposed to the privileges of others.

A common missionary failing, or perhaps it is a common female failing, is to fuss over our lack of gifts, as though God had sent us out to do a job without the proper equipment. I have spent far too much time regretting my awkward temperament, wishing I was like Susie, and wanting gifts that God has given to John. I often exhorted a

---

[1] *Gold by Moonlight*

friend who is given to this kind of wishing: "Look, if God wanted you to have Susie's temperament He would have given it to you. If your work for Him required gifts like John's, He would have given them to you." I was very emphatic about it, for I could see clearly how my friend needed to change her views. It was much more difficult to change my own. For underlying this longing to be someone else was a dislike of myself displayed in a thriving inferiority complex. I could never work hard enough to compensate for it, and I needed the constant bolstering of my companions' appreciation. Weeks could go by with no one noticing anything about me to be appreciated! Thus I spent considerable time exploring the murky unpleasant depths of the Slough of Despond.

There was still a wide gap between my theology, which told me I was loved and accepted by God, and my experience of that truth. Through many years the Lord was working to close the gap, and the day came when I *knew* what I had known all along — that I was accepted in the Beloved. I was freed to believe in and rejoice in His complete forgiveness and His total love. The compulsive urge for perfection in all things could be thankfully abandoned. It had been a great strain, for I never attained perfection in anything, nor had I recognized that some of my good works were undertaken with the hope of deserving sanctification. Sanctification is His work. He, the Sovereign God, has predestined me — silly and sinful as I am

— to be conformed to the likeness of his Son. It is sheer relief to hand over the responsibility to Him, and great joy to know He is pledged to finish in me the work He has begun. Yes, He is the perfect teacher of theology.

Usually in my daily Bible reading I study short passages in detail, but lately I have been reading quickly through ten to fifteen chapters at a time, and I have been amazed at the insight that comes from the range of Scripture. Isaiah and Jeremiah leave you in no doubt as to the sovereignty of God. The New International Version uses the term "the sovereign Lord", and this truth is reinforced with each repetition of "Thus saith the Lord." Over and over again comes reassurance. "My purpose will stand and I will do all that I please... What I have said, that will I do... My mouth has uttered in all integrity a word that will not be revoked... The Lord Almighty has sworn. Surely as I have planned, so will it be, and as I have purposed so it will stand... The sovereign Lord will wipe away the tears from all faces; the Lord has spoken." That is what He says in His textbook. Then He sends me out for practical application of the truth, so that I will know He is the One who manages my affairs, even everyday ones.

I remember when we were planning our first move to a Lahu village. There seemed to be a conspiracy to keep us from getting there, for it was one delay after another. In the end, as we were still firmly rooted in Chiang Rai and Larry had promised to be with the Lahu Christians over Christmas, he went off on his own to do his duty. That holiday was so lonely without him. I made things outwardly as festive as possible for Marilyn and Shirley, but inwardly I needed cheering up myself. I could not understand why the Lord had not arranged things more efficiently, so that we could have been together as a family with the Lahu. Then Larry came home with the news that the entire village had decided to move to another location, some miles north on another mountain, with everything having to be carried on someone's back or on the very few ponies the villagers possessed. And if I had had my way about the timing of our move to the village, we would have had to abandon our tribal house and move all our stuff too.

For a time I had forgotten that "faith is exceedingly charitable and believeth no evil of God."[2] Now I felt so ashamed of my irritation with the Lord, and thankful He had spared us this double trauma. I should have trusted Him, for His holiness and wisdom and love are all part of His sovereignty. He chose us before the creation of the world to be holy and blameless in His sight, so He chooses circumstances that will ensure our growth in grace. Every parcel He sends is wrapped in love. To believe this, to *know* this, is a complete safeguard against bitterness, cynicism and worry. Andrew Murray has said, "He has the power to

---

[2]Samuel Rutherford.

make our circumstances, however difficult, a heavenly discipline, a gain and a blessing. He has taken them all up into the life plan He has for us as Redeemer. Did we but believe this we should gladly meet every event with the worship of an adoring faith."[3]

[3]*Holiest of All.*

Chapter 22

Lord, Teach Us To Pray!

THE HMONG DESPERATELY needed a well, and prayed earnestly about its location. There was not much in the way of natural clues but they finally agreed on a spot and prayed together again before they dug their small test place, a round hole about five inches across and fifteen inches deep. In the evening dry leaves were placed at the bottom of the hole, and in the morning the undersides of the leaves were wet. While the ladies prayed the men dug, but the ground was dry. They kept digging through the arid soil and found nothing. Had they been mistaken after all? In discouragement they were ready to quit, but someone said, "Let's give it one more try," and they picked up their shovels and went at it again. At last a trickle of water appeared, and there was great rejoicing. It turned out to be a good well and never went dry, even in the dry season when lack of water is such a problem.

Today in North Thailand there are many tribal Christians who can testify to the fact that God listens as they pray. As God has taught them we too have been refreshed, and have rejoiced with them in the answers to their prayers. They do not, as we often do, divorce "Christian" activity from "making a living" activity. They know God is interested in their rice crops and the welfare of the pigs as well as in their efforts to learn to read His Word and to walk in obedience.

We missionaries can also testify to the fact that we have a prayer-answering God. Doe Jones had been ill with suspected hepatitis and two missionary friends wanted to visit her mountain village and give some tender loving care. Their backpacks were bulging with nourishing food for the patient, and they needed someone to carry the packs and show the way. No one could be found until late in the morning, when an opium sot who wanted to get opium in the mountains consented to be carrier and guide. With a backpack on either end of a carrying pole he led the way for two hours and then, exhausted, sank to the ground and said he could go no further. It was probably true, for opium smokers have limited strength and limited perseverance. What were the ladies to do? They could neither go ahead or turn back, for mountain trails are tricky and boast no traffic signs. They sat down on a tree trunk to pray. As they prayed they heard some commotion, and when they had finished and looked up they saw an elephant! Where were they going? they asked the riders. To Doe's village, to drag in logs. Would they be willing to take the backpacks? Yes, if it didn't matter that they would not arrive in the village until next morning.

The carrier, relieved of his loads, had a new burst of energy and started off confidently to lead the way. But it was a miserably steep path, and then it began to rain. He was soon repenting of his willingness to guide, and as they slogged along in mud or slipped on the shiny path the girls did everything but actually carry him up the mountain. When evening came they stumbled wearily along in the dark, thankfully reaching Doe's house at 8 p.m. They wondered if they would ever see the backpacks again, but next morning they were safely delivered to Doe's door according to the agreement.

Elephants don't just roam around the jungle. Who arranged for one to be at that particular spot on the trail at that particular time? And that the drivers would be going to Doe's village... and would be both agreeable and honest — a combination not easily found? Later the ladies heard that the elephant did no log pulling, just carried up their backpacks and went down again. God made those arrangements in answer to prayer but He didn't transport that elephant to the needed place in a twinkling of an eye. Before they called He answered. He anticipated their need. If we need an elephant He can supply one.

Most of our needs are less exotic. When we lived in a small village near the foot of the Lahu mountains, our only fuel was charcoal. In our inexperience we had not realized that once the rains came on we would not be able to find charcoal, and should have bought in a big supply before the rainy season began. Larry went searching but could not find any anywhere, and feeling his trip had been in vain he started for home, praying as he cycled. Suddenly from a house he was passing he heard a voice calling out, "Do you want to buy some charcoal?" He was able to order what we needed and next morning an oxcart load of charcoal came to our door. Coincidence? Perhaps. But every missionary can tell you of such "coincidences" and can rejoice in the prayer-answering God who arranges them.

OMF first had contact with the Pwo Karen in 1954, and in the years that followed, as missionaries learned the language, a wide area was evangelized. It was hard work toiling up mountains hot under the glare of the sun. Missionaries lived in Karen villages but saw little to encourage them. The Karen were interested in money and medicine, but heaven was far off and who could know who would get there? In the meantime the spirits had to be propitiated and the rice planted. We prayed but saw little answer. A few Karen believed, but the work appeared to be at a dead end.

In our annual conference in 1974 we considered the Karen field and asked ourselves, "Is OMF still responsible for this unresponsive tribe?" Messages on the life of Abraham had stimulated our faith and the field agreed that we could not write off the Karen work, so we pledged special prayer for the tribe and for Jim and Louise Morris as they returned to it. Outwardly there was nothing to indicate that a breakthrough was at hand. However, for some time one Karen family had maintained a Christian witness, and a month after our conference some of their relatives believed. We began to see God at work in Karen lives, and the year of special prayer thrust was a year of blessing.

We had prayed before and had not seen blessing — that is, we had not seen visible evidence of God's working. But He was at work. Those twenty years of costly witness, and the prayers that accompanied the giving of the Gospel, were all part of the total picture. The good news had to be preached by God's messengers, supported by the prayers of His people. Then came a special concentration of prayer and the time for God to act openly. I do not know how to explain the mystery of prayer and the timing of God's answers. He answers according to the need that He sees, which may be different from the need that *we* see. However, there are some things I do know. God acts at the right time — the appointed time — what Paul refers to as the fullness of time. God is never dilatory, never late. There is a divine timetable, and when we pray we can trust this aspect of His sovereignty.

I have puzzled, as we all have, over the relation of prayer to God's sovereignty and man's free will. Someone has said that paradoxes resemble the opposite sides of a mountain. I can see only one side of the mountain at a time. If I am viewing man's free will I feel it to be at variance with God's sovereignty. If I contemplate the side of the mountain that represents His sovereignty I will not see the side that represents my will, my prayers. However, from an airplane I might be able to see there is just one mountain with views in opposite directions. God sees one mountain, and if He has commanded me to pray then I am not to be put off by theological puzzles.

It was probably in the early months of 1954 that Akermeema first heard of the Lord. At the time when Edna McLaren and Eileen Kuhn (then O'Rourke) were in her Lisu village, Akermeema was a second wife, out of favor and of little importance to her husband, Headman Honey. The ladies sometimes stayed in her house and when I visited with Eileen I stayed there too. Akermeema was lonely and to be pitied. She wanted to respond to the Gospel but was too fearful of her husband to be a Christian openly. Headman Honey had no time for a foreign religion, and did not want others in his village believing either. His wife knew he was a hard man and that tribal beatings are merciless. In June 1956 the North Thailand field agreed to pray for Honey's conversion, but shortly after that his village moved and regrouped in the way tribal villages do, and the missionaries lost track of them. In 1961 Edna and a friend found Akermeema again, a real answer to prayer as they had been trying for months to locate her. She was noncommittal when asked about her relationship with the Lord, but did seem to appreciate reading from the Word and prayer. Because of my interest in Akermeema I continued to pray for her and her husband, and so did others.

It was October 1974 when missionaries on the Lisu mountains again found Akermeema and her husband. This time they were "found" by the Lord too, and with Headman Honey believing Akermeema was also free to follow the Lord. Did you notice those dates? It was almost twenty years from the first prayers for Headman Honey until the day God answered. God was not absent in those years. He was showing Honey his deep need, and in His grace He gave the man another opportunity to enter into life. A very short time after this we heard of Honey's death. His first wife continues to believe but Akermeema is wandering.

In these days of instant coffee and instant success, anything that takes time wearies us. We get tired of praying much sooner than the Lord tires of listening to us. I have read many books explaining why the answer is delayed, but none of them satisfy me, and I have now come to the place of accepting the fact that we may have to pray for a long time. God has said that I am not to faint, I am not to feel weary as though I cannot go on any longer. There is one request that I have prayed for over forty years. I see no sign of an answer, but I refuse to stop. At times I have to be honest with the Lord and say, "Lord, you know I wonder if my prayer will ever be answered. I don't pray with faith that is bolstered by any outward sign that the answer is near. I feel like stopping, but you have said to pray and I want to obey you so I make this request once again." I have a small book in which

I record prayers in one column and answers in another, and this is a grand stimulus to faith. But there are blank places still to be filled in. When we know as we are known, how much of intended blessing will we find has been held back by the double locked doors of doubt and prayerlessness?

One December a friend wrote saying, "My Christmas gift to you is this: I will pray daily for you for the next year." It was the best present I ever received, and I cannot say how much encouragement it brought, to say nothing of the benefit of her prayers. God has given to us in the OMF a great supportive group of such people. When in our home countries on furlough we would try to visit the prayer bands that pray specially for OMF missionaries, which are often made up of little old ladies. We thank God for them, but can't help wondering who will take over their prayer work, for one by one our prayer helpers are going Home. This is not surprising in that I am fast approaching the "little old lady" category myself! I thoroughly protest the notion that prayer is a duty incumbent only upon the elderly and infirm, as though the Lord had said, "Ye aged, pray the Lord of the harvest for laborers," or "When you are old, you must pray and not faint." The commands to pray are addressed to all people who know the Lord, irrespective of age.

One lady in such a group didn't have much to say during the preliminary chitchat and we hadn't particularly noticed her. But when she began to pray we noticed. She was a prayer partner for one of our Bangkok missionaries who at that time lived with a group of Thai students. She knew their names, though not how to pronounce them — but the Lord recognized who was meant! — and she prayed in detail over their problems and rejoiced over the victories God had given them. As far as I know she had never met any Thai people and certainly had never seen these lads, but she knew them through prayer. I thought of the joy it will be when she meets, in Heaven, the boys she helped to pray there. Prayer links us with His work.

I have to admit that I have found the writing of this book painfully soul-searching. I am daring to ask for prayer, I who do so little praying myself. I remember the Lord's stern word about people who "teach" and don't "do", when the divine order is "do" and then "teach." But I take courage from the fact that if Christians were to wait for personal perfection in the subject they want to teach, no one would write or say another word. I am a fellow learner in prayer, sharing things that concern those of us who desire to please God.

William Law wrote, "You see two persons; one is regular in public and private prayer, the other is not. Now the reason of this difference is not this —that one has strength and power to observe prayer; but the reason is this — that one intends to please God in the duties of devotion and the other has no intention about it."[1] Prayer involves a

---

[1] *A Serious Call to a Devout Life*

conscious choice. We are prone to think that our lack of prayer is due to what a friend calls a "dizzy-busy" life. There are so many demands made on us — with such pressured days we surely cannot be faulted for our prayerlessness. This attitude helps us overlook the truth that, rather than being pressured by duties almost beyond our control, we have actually *chosen* to fill our lives with other things.

It was nearly twenty years ago that I wrote in a letter, "Lord, teach us to pray! No one can be complacent about the slowness of the work in North Thailand. If such slowness is God's full plan for us now then we don't want to miss any of His disciplinary lessons, for there is much to be learned in a period of 'non-success.' But we need to be sensitive to know when the Lord would lead us out into definite expectant prayer for a larger manifest working of His Spirit. May we not be content when the Lord wants us to be 'desperate.' He can teach us our prayer attitude for each tribal situation." I echo those words today because we still stand in great need of lessons in prayer.

Our personalities often dictate our prayer concerns. I myself am a melancholic, an "Eeyore." Eeyores tend to note every unhappy detail, the inconsistencies of the local believers, their incredible slowness to take new steps of faith. If this leads us to prayer, that is good, but it can turn to a sort of spiritual misanthropy that is deadly, for it does not remember the Lord and takes the hope out of prayer. The Pollyannas stand in direct contrast to this. We have a cheerful Pollyanna-ish friend who is capable of saying in the middle of an earthquake, "Isn't this the nicest shaking up you have ever had?" Pollyannas view every discouraging situation in the best possible light, and find it easy to praise God. But rose-tinted glasses may obscure issues that should be dealt with, situations that need changing by prayer. Incidentally, if you put a Pollyanna and an Eeyore to work together and listen to their reports and their prayers, you may well wonder if they are talking about the same area!

God has made both melancholics and sanguines, so He will use both to reveal aspects of His grace. He does not want to destroy personality, but He wants us to be so related to Him that we can view things from His standpoint. He alone sees things as they truly are. He does not gloss over imperfections, or exaggerate, or give trivialities undue importance. He knows what He is going to do about each situation, and He asks us to work together with Him. In each situation we need to ask, "Should we be restful, waiting to see the eventual display of your power? Or should we be intensely concerned, taking up the weapons of warfare you have provided?" It is tragic to be content when we should be desperate.

At this time in our North Thailand history we need both missionaries and prayer helpers with undistorted vision, who clearly see God before they see the problems. There are reasons for encouragement, but the devil is not idle. He is specially busy in the lives of tribal Christians who, not truly enjoying the Lord's presence nor living in His power, are counting the cost of discipleship. To them the old life appears more attractive than it once did. This is God's call to prayer! I cannot believe that these thirty years of "blood, sweat and tears" are for nothing, that it is all going to peter out. God began the work and He will finish it. Perhaps the present doldrums are to remind us of our own helplessness. Our aims may be high, our motives sincere, and our methods good, but *we* cannot produce saints. "Therefore we resolutely turn our eyes away from our all too obvious impotence and rest in His proved competence," wrote the CIM directors as the mission moved into new areas after leaving China. "We are at the end of our resources, but His infinite resources remain unexhausted. It is apparent that the staggering need of S.E.Asia can be met only by a supernatural manifestation of divine power and presence — a movement in the spiritual realm comparable to an earthquake in the physical — a movement which will cause the mountains to flow down at His presence. We will therefore continue in importunate prayer for such an outpouring of the Spirit until it is granted." Lord, teach us to pray.

Indeed we need to be both taught and enabled. We naturally shrink from the taxing demands of a prayer ministry. It takes strength, physical and spiritual, and the sacrificial use of time. You don't drift into such a ministry. It is not glamorous or exciting. It is not seen or commended by the public. Only God knows those who have prayerful hearts.

A friend from North Thailand recently wrote telling how God was helping her to pray. She said that when she did not know how to frame petitions for a baffling situation, she remembered that the Lord Jesus was already praying for these matters. She then could say, "I join in your prayers, Lord Jesus. I add my 'amen' to whatever you are praying for the church." He, the Son of God, ever lives to make intercession for His people. He is the Great Intercessor who lives within us, and if we ask He will empower us to respond to His invitation to share His prayer concerns.